DEAD MEAT

KYLE WRIGHT

JOURNALSTONE
YOUR LINK TO ARTIST TALENT

ISBN: 978-1-68510-098-8 (sc)
ISBN: 978-1-68510-099-5 (ebook)
Library of Congress Catalog Number: 2023939168

First printing edition June 9, 2023
Published by JournalStone Publishing in the United States of America.
Cover Artwork and Design: Don Noble
Edited by Sean Leonard
Proofreading and Cover/Interior Layout by Scarlett R. Algee

JournalStone Publishing
3205 Sassafras Trail
Carbondale, Illinois 62901

JournalStone books may be ordered through booksellers or by contacting:
JournalStone | www.journalstone.com

This one's for you, Jenna Marie. Thanks for breathing life into Harry Ypsilanti when he was just a bunch of weird words on the page.

All Cats Are Beautiful.

DEAD MEAT

1

"THIS IS A true story—for real this time, not some Hollywood version of a true story, with all the bits changed until it's just the bland outer shell of truth left in the picture—of one sleepy town and its people. A story of the last grips of summer, sun shining off dull pearl of sidewalks and the windows of houses. The easy charm of knowing your neighbor, of a slow contemplative pace, relishing the small things and the quiet moments. It's just another town, like any other. Like yer's maybe. Or not. Either way, she's had her ups and downs. The seagull explosion back in the twenties. Them kids went missing out by the cannibal's house. All the weird moss growin on any wood surface in town, no matter how much you spray and scrape. Nothing out of the ordinary, though. Forest Rapids has had its share of good things too. The annual town chili cook-off, whoa boy. Forest Rapids is also the birthplace of Freddy's Fabulous Foot Cream, and Dergible Grover, noted actor recognized for his memorable death on an episode of *The Rifleman*.

"But this shinin city's been down in the dumps of late. Before the war, this city had such a…magic. Now, somethin just feels off. It's kinda startin ta feel like a murky bog in this place, a stagnant little sewage reservoir. Somethin's wrong in Forest Rapids, and it's gettin worse every day."

A large, ill-shaven man, red-eyed, wearing wrinkled clothes, sits at a desk, a cigarette streaming smoke into the lamplight before him. He is stout, and looks like he's been hit in the face more than a few times with a large stick. All of his features—eyes, nose, even his lips—somehow feel…slightly bent. He stares expectantly at a younger woman sitting across from him, stiffly staring ahead. They are both silent. The clock ticks, soft clacking above the loud whir of the ceiling fan. The man clears his throat.

"Oh, um…uh," the woman begins, unsure what to say to any of the man's rambling, somewhat incoherent story. She leans out of the plume of his cigarette smoke. It follows her. She is short with hardened features, thin lines along the edges of her face like highlights on a drawing. She clears her throat. Sweat beads her brow, and the woman leans forward into Harry's piercing stare, holding his gaze.

"So, Miss Brandt, what'd ya think? If they was gonna make a movie of my life, that's prolly how I'd start it. Cagney or Bogie, a semi-darkened office, shots of late afternoon shadows, intercut with me—them—talkin, and maybe like a shot of a sewage pipe burbalin shit-water near the end, right? Like when I'm sayin, 'stagnate little sewage reservoir,' it's, y'know…*showin* it."

"Uh…it was very, uh…cinematic." What the hell else was she supposed to say to that? For a minute or two into this guy's monologue, she wasn't even sure if he worked here, or if he was just some crazy come stumbling in off the street. Was this guy really the one who ran this place? Jesus.

"Ya think? Great. So ya really wanna work here, huh? Why da hell would ya want ta do that?" the man asks, almost as if he could read her thoughts. He sits back in his chair. "I mean, this job ain't all good looks and fast times, y'know? It's life or death out there sometimes. Even in a small city like this."

"Well, yes, I do want to work for you. I've always wanted to be a police officer…and I *was*, when all the fellas went off to war. But after they all came home, I was let go." The woman says this carefully, keeping her tone neutral. So hard to keep her voice soft, the edge of her words from cutting. All the bitterness, the bile she stamped down. All the pulses of rage flaring and being forced back somewhere. Whirring through every part of her.

"Let go?"

"Yes, the men came back, and needed their jobs back…and there just wasn't enough room for me." Keep the face neutral, keep the eyes level, steady. Don't let the tone turn dark. Don't let the violence inside get out. Don't mess this interview up too. Can't have a repeat of the Donut Shop interview…

"Cause you're a woman," the man says more than asks. The woman's eyes flash volcanic coals, then back to steady. "Fuckin pricks. Hell, for all they know yer worth two a them boys…and knowin Ol Captain Dickie Boy and his shit kickers over there, yer prolly worth three of em."

"I was let go with full merits and a generous review. I don't think—"

"Ha! Ya did good, kid, just not good enough to stay. Have a swell time now… Those fuckin guys… Well, my psychotherapist tells me I'm an 'alcoholic' and a 'dangerous risk-taker,' whatever the hell that means. We're like two peas in a pod. C'mon, kid, let's go."

The woman wrinkles her nose at this, her eyes widening a little. "Oh, uh…"

The man stands up, puts on a long trench coat hanging from a rack near the door, and pushes his way outside. The woman follows him. Okay, so…nothing weird about any of this, right?

A battered Cadillac Series Sixty-One, once emerald-colored, is parked near the curb, slightly crooked. The man attempts to open the passenger door, finally giving it a swift kick, and it groans as it swings outward.

"C'mon, kid… Lorene, right? Hop in, and try not to track any dirt inside," the man says, motioning into the grimy car's even more disgusting interior.

"So…I got the job?"

"I'm not big on labels and generalizations, you'll come to find that out." With that, Harry shoves his huge frame into the driver's seat.

Inside the car, the seats appear to be burned, shot, slashed, blood-stained, and covered in various other unidentifiable splatters and splotches. Trash litters the floor: empty cigarette packs, bottles, cans—some of them beer—rolling paper wrappers, loose slips of crumpled paper. Donut wrappers stuck to the floor and the leather seats, and an Abba Zabba bar stuck to the roof of the car, sun-faded and frozen in a half-drip, sugar stalactite.

Awkward silence fills the crevices in the car as it barrels down one of the town's outlying roads, turning into cornfields and empty gaps between the houses. No one in sight. Silence reverberates off the inside of the windshield, fills the empty sandwich wrappers on the floor. Begins to seep into Lorene's pores, making it harder to move her mouth, to make words.

"Huh?!" Harry bellows suddenly, silence tattered, awkwardness heightened.

"Uh…I didn't say anything."

"Oh." Harry nods as if satisfied.

"Uh…"

"Huh? Well, we're just about here, kid," Harry mutters in his thick accent, which Lorene can't seem to place. Like Brooklyn mixed with Kentucky, or some kind of French mixed with a dialect from New Jersey…

Harry turns off the road into the long driveway of some kind of factory or industrial building.

"And *here* is…?"

The car weaves around large potholes that threaten to swallow the sizeable vehicle with little effort, Harry saying nothing. In front of the building, he finally shuts the engine off. Busted-out windows, what little grass there was around the place overgrown and dying, brown and bamboo-colored. The white-painted metal door hangs limply on rusted hinges.

"Our first case."

"Huh?"

"What you asked earlier, y'know, 'And here is…' after I said—"

"Yes, I got that, I meant *huh* as in, this is our first case? This abandoned factory on the asshole edge of town?"

"Oh, man, asshole edge, I'm writin that one down in my book. I got a notebook I keep with good ideas and such, good one-liners I quip before beatin the tar outta some baddie…stuff like that. That one is definitely goin in there. Anyway, just follow my lead." Harry quickly scribbles in a small notepad he has pulled from his pocket. When he replaces it, Lorene notices a telegram sticking from the pocket, and the word **URGENT** typed boldly across its top.

"Aren't you going to, you know, give me some information? Procedures, maybe? Like, an orientation or something?" Harry is digging through the trash in the backseat. Maybe this isn't such a good idea. Her brother had recommended Harry, they had served together during the war, but… Ashley was a bit crazy after he came back from over there…and this guy seemed absolutely nutso! Maybe she should just take that job typing at Jackson, Johnson, and Jasons. *How bad could old Mr. Jasons really be?*

"Ew!" Harry squeals, pulling his hand from the garbage pile he has been rifling through. Something neon-green glows on his fingertips, dripping slowly, thickly down onto the floor of the car. Harry wipes his hand on his coat.

"So?" Lorene asks, just a hint of the anger bubbling just below the surface roiling up into her words before she stamps it back down.

"So what?! I just gave you the procedures. 'Follow my lead!' Got it?"

"Uh, no, not—"

"Good. C'mon, kid, duty calls."

Moment of truth. Stay or go. Follow this asshole into an abandoned factory, possibly to be serial-killer butchered, or just leave now and be chased off from another job by some misogynistic prick. No. Screw that. Let's see what this loony toon has in store.

Lorene follows Harry to the doorway.

"What are we doing? Is this—"

"Our first case," Harry says, reaching into his trenchcoat. His hand comes out clutching a small revolver with a gold design along the barrel. "Ya got a gun, kid?"

"Uh, like, on me? No."

"Damn. Shoulda got one back at the shop. Meh…probably won't need it anyway."

"What the hell? What do you mean?!"

"You'll be fine. If you have to, you know, if the shootin starts, just…you know…kill someone that got a gun…then you got a gun!" Harry smiles broadly. "Here goes."

"Wait, what—?"

Before Lorene can finish, Harry gives the door a swift boot, more limber than she ever would have given him credit for, and the hinges groan unhappily as the metal slab flies inward. Two men are standing inside the empty building. They both stare at Harry and Lorene as they enter. One of the men is holding a black leather briefcase, the other some sort of animal carrier.

"Fellas, put down the items in your hands and put them into the air," Harry says in a surprisingly intelligible voice. The two men comply, setting down what they hold.

"Who the fuck are you?" one of the men asks.

"Harry Ypsilanti, PI. We're here on behalf of the owner of that cat. Sorry, boys, I can't let ya leave with her."

"Oh, a fuckin PI?! They ain't even cops, Ronnie!" the other man shouts as both draw pistols and begin firing, laughing hysterically. Harry and Lorene dive for cover behind a large crate.

"You boys're gonna regret this," Harry calls, gruffly.

"You'll never take us alive, gumshoes!"

A shot zips from above them and strikes the ground at Lorene's feet. A third man has appeared on the catwalk overlooking the factory floor. Harry fires up at him, and the man screams loudly and topples over. Blood drips down through the mesh of the catwalk. A lot of blood, it seems to Lorene…*too much*, her mind screams briefly. No time to think on that.

"You doin okay, kid?" Harry asks, almost drowned out by the sound of gunfire. Before Lorene can answer, Harry spins around the stack of boxes they are hiding behind and fires toward the two remaining shooters. He hits one of the men, who falls mutely. The other takes careful aim, and hits Harry's gun hand. Blood and chunks of flesh spray everywhere as Harry falls back behind the boxes. Lorene is pelted with something gooey and hard, maybe a fingertip with a nail still attached, she can't tell. As Harry lies spasming in front of her, the remaining shooter takes off running, briefcase in hand. Lorene doesn't hesitate and grabs Harry's Colt Commando Revolver from a pile of gore on the concrete in front of her. One of his fingers still cradles the trigger. A deep breath, square aim at the back of the running man's head, Lorene squeezes the trigger gently—

The man flies forward, swept off his feet. Something's not right…a moment of confusion Lorene can't quite put her finger on. Something in the bullet's heft didn't feel right.

"They all dead, kid?" Harry asks, sitting up. His wrist is ragged and pink and spurting fluids like a yard hose. He wraps a small piece of cloth around his stump, the blood still pulsing through it like a coffee filter. "You okay?"

"I don't know. Are *you* okay?! We need to get you to a hospital!"

"I'll be all right. Let's grab the cat, get the hell outta here. 'Fore the fuzz shows up," Harry says, standing slowly. He brushes himself off with his remaining hand, then saunters over to the cat carrier and picks it up. He tries to wipe some of the blood from the side of it with his coat, but the jagged wound at his wrist splashes more of it back onto the carrier.

"Time to go, kid," Harry says flatly. Lorene looks overwhelmed, but her eyes harden. Tears stop just as they begin forming. Her brows pull taut, low on her face. Her mouth closes, tightens, draws itself thinner.

"All right."

A gunshot crackles and rings, echoes in the now-silent enclosed space. Blood sprays from Harry's chest across Lorene's face. She screams and begins firing on one of the men on the ground, who is sitting upright, holding a pistol in one hand and his own bloody side with the other. Lorene's shot strikes the man and he falls. Shoulda been a better shot, got him in the head—?

Thought falters, eyes bring wrong readings—

No one else moves, the scent of salt and burnt wood in the air. Fireworks. The animal in the carrier shifts, mews quietly.

2

MUSICAL NOTES IN the silence. Parade of voices. Lorene feels the excited pattering of her heartbeat. Blood rushing through her veins, muscles, the crevices of her brain. Feeling her meat fill with it, awash in the racing fluid. What to do…what to do…?

Lorene approaches the cat carrier cautiously. She peeks through the bars, and the mewing stops. A small, fuzzy, wide-eyed cat sits staring back at her, motionless.

"Hey there, little buddy. Are you okay?" Lorene asks softly. The cat mews a response and blinks her eyes at Lorene. "Okay…what the hell do I do now, kitty cat?"

Lorene looks over at Harry's lifeless body, slumped over on the floor in a growing pool of blood. It looks just like the movies, fake and bright. *I thought it'd be more…*real *looking…* Lorene notices the note sticking from Harry's breast pocket again, spackled only lightly in gore. She reaches for it. Slowly. Cautiously. A dripping from somewhere in the room, might be blood. A car horn from outside, blaring and screaming past rapidly.

The note is a telegram from a Mr. Delaware Jackson, asking for the help of "the famed and dashing (?) private investigator, Harry Ypsilanti" in retrieving his prized cat, Chesterfield, who was stolen from him.

"Chesterfield, like the cigarettes? Okay." Lorene says to the cat inside the carrier. The cat squeaks back at the sound of her name. "Well, Mr. Jackson seems to have left an address. I guess we should at least get you home. Finish the case, right?"

As Lorene picks up the cat carrier, a slow, steady, wet-sounding clapping begins next to her. She whirls around, Harry's pistol at the ready. Harry is sitting up, smiling and slapping his stump on the forearm of his other, still-intact hand.

"Harry, holy shit! I thought you were—are you—we gotta get you to—"

"You did it, kid."

"What?!" Lorene doesn't lower the pistol. Her body tenses back up. None of this adds up: the setting, the gunfight, all that blood…too much blood…too red. The strange note. All this over a cat…

"You did it! You passed!"

"What are you talking about?"

"The interview, kid, you did it! I had to be sure, don't ya see? Ya passed! Boys, boys, go ahead and get up!" Harry stands and begins walking toward Lorene, whose face is contorted somewhere between tears and shouting. The fingers of her left hand clench to a fist, her right hand tightens around the gun. No thoughts pass her brain, just images of bodily pain, of hurting someone. Flashes of tearing Harry limb from limb. Flashes of other assholes she's had to put up with. She sees her fists raising up, striking Harry, first in his extended gut, then right in the bridge of his nose. They keep coming. Blood responds, real blood this time. Darker, thicker, not for show.

Lorene's fingers clench and unclench almost rhythmically. The dead men in the room sit up. Lorene lets out a quick yelp and fires at one of them.

"Hey, hey! Easy, now, easy! You shootin blanks, kid."

Lorene stops firing and Harry gently takes the pistol from her hands. The three men approach cautiously, covered in drying blood.

"I, uh…" Lorene struggles to form words above gurgles, struggles to keep her legs straight, struggles to keep upright.

"May I present three of Forest Rapids' finest stage actors," Harry says, and the three men bow theatrically.

"But…" Lorene begins, looking to Harry's stump, blood still dribbling out in sporadic gulps.

"Oh, this? Special effects, y'know? It's amazing what they can do nowadays, for movies and such." Harry pushes his hand through the stump, ripping rubber and foam and splashing the last of the blood-like liquid onto the floor. He drops the broken prop and wiggles his fingers, pleased with himself. "It was the final part a' tha interview. I had ta see how you'd hold up under pressure, and if you'd get the job done, no matter what. You did it, kid. Real good. You got the job, hands down…no pun intended."

Harry extends his slick hand toward Lorene. She stares at it for a moment.

"What the fuck? Just, what the fuck? You enormous creep! Do you do this to all your potential employees?" Lorene suddenly explodes. "Of all the stupid, irresponsible things—" she begins…what words does she even use? How to even start to express everything going on inside her head right now verbally. She glares at Harry, who nods slowly.

"As a matter a fact, I do run this simulation for all perspective employees. The few times I've had em."

"Who the hell do you think you are?! Someone could have gotten hurt!"

"Sorry, kid, it's just the way of the job. I'd do the same thing if you were a strapping young lad comin offa da football squad, or a Marine come back from the war, or General Patton himself. It don't reflect on you, or you bein…female and all. Everybody gets the same treatment with Harry Ypsilanti. Whatever bits you got or might not got, whatever color your bits are, whoever you like to touch bits with, we all the same in my book."

Lorene is silent, eyes radiating red heat, her scowl growing razor edges, not really hearing whatever it is Harry's babbling about. Still trying not to throttle Ypsilanti's throat with her bare hands. Thinking about that slick, chubby flesh squeezed between her fingers, the gargle he'd make.

"So I take it that's you declinin the job offer then, right?"

Lorene pauses a moment, not taking her eyes off Harry's. Just one more asshole… We aren't scared of him. We are stronger than him, and we won't be chased away from this too.

"When do I start?"

"You already did, Miss Brandt. You already did. Welcome to the company."

* * *

Harry and Lorene fester in the silence in the car. Harry drives, a constipated look on his face.

"Okay, kid… Sorry again about back there. Maybe that isn't, you know, best business practices. But *this* case's the real deal. Some dame says her husband's gone missing. Doesn't too much like the fuzz, so she called me."

Lorene doesn't say anything. She has been thinking about what to say to all this since they had left the warehouse, dropping the cat near Harry's office, driving through the nearly empty midday streets. A few scattered people watering lawns, walking dogs. A young boy pedals by on his bicycle, brown-leather helmeted head looking like a rotting apple about to split open.

The house is a small modular home, with an immaculately trimmed and watered front yard, beautiful explosion of multi-colored wildflowers up along the base of the faint-blue linoleum. Harry parks the car in front of the house.

"Okay, kid, no tricks this time. Let's see what this one's all about."

At the front door, Harry knocks slowly, loudly. Thick meaty raps, but with a cadence, a musicality, that keeps them from sounding too much like the insistent pounding of a cop.

A woman in her early sixties answers the door. Her eyes are red and wet, as if she has been crying. She sniffles and eyes the two people on her porch suspiciously.

"Gretchen Marsh?"

"Yes…?"

"I'm the private investigator you called—"

"Oh, Mr…Yepatlantis?"

"Uh, Ypsilanti, ma'am. Harry Ypsilanti. And this is my associate, Lorene Brandt. May we come in?"

"Oh, uh…I'd rather not. Maybe we can do this out here…in the fresh air. It's such a lovely day out here." Gretchen shifts anxiously, closes the door behind her before Harry responds. He and Lorene exchange a brief look.

"Sure, Mrs. Marsh. So you say your husband didn't come home after work last night?" Harry asks, pulling out a pen and notepad.

"That's correct. I don't know where he is! Please, if something terrible hasn't happened to him…then he's up to something…that Mariam down at the VFW hall is always givin my Phillip the eye… I bet it's her…"

"I think that might just be on account of one of her eyes bein glass, but what do I know. Anyway, so this is either foul play or a lover's foul. Luckily, we do both. As we discussed over the telephone, Mrs. Marsh, my fee is $100 per day, plus expenses incurred…and we will find your husband, one way or the other."

"I know you had said that, but jeez, that seems a little steep to me, Mr. Yopsudenko."

"Ypsilanti…and you're payin fer the best. Thirty years a expertise at your disposal here." Harry smiles broadly at himself.

"Well…all right then. Just please help me find my husband."

"No problem, ma'am. Harry Ypsilanti and Associates are on the case. First things first, though. We do need to take a look inside your home, see if there are any clues, anything amiss…use our keen detective eyes to see if there's anything you may not have noticed."

Gretchen looks pained. "Oh, um… If you gotta. Let's go, I guess. Just, uh, watch your step, you know. The place is a bit of a mess at the moment, I didn't have time to tidy up or anything."

Gretchen opens the door and leads them inside. A stench hits Lorene's nose before she can see anything. A garbage dump, but worse. A garbage box. With your face in it. A dumpster Halloween mask. Organic rot, bodily smells, fecal and warm and feeling like they're crawling sickly inside her nose, some creep at the bar she can't ditch. Rotten flakes in the air like bad snow. Chemical smells too; not cleaner or chemicals to fight the other odors, more like the spot of town by the steel and paper mills on the river, foul and choking. Then she registers the sights. Piles of old magazines and newspapers stacked like an entryway on either side of the door. Old pizza boxes, fast food wrappers. Piles of clothes, a dozen or so each of every kind of kitchen utensil one could think of, still tagged with price stickers, crammed into the corner among a pile of various single shoes and broken vinyl records, snapped and jagged and smiling pointy-toothed grins. Stacks of fabric shards and moldering paper. Books everywhere. Yellowing, blackening, some already falling into mush. Too many Bibles for Lorene to count. Multiple ashtrays overflowing with cigarette butts. Something shifts next to Lorene. The smell of an animal den and a detergent factory...on fire. Lorene sees a row of twisted wheelchairs missing seats, missing wheels, next to a collection of bent and twisted hubcaps, all manner of sizes and designs and states of warp and rust.

Gretchen leads them weaving through a maze, along a trail in a cluttered forest of refuse and psychologically damaged consumerism.

'Uh, maybe the bedroom, Mrs. Marsh? We may find something there." Harry turns away from Gretchen and wrinkles his nose in disgust to Lorene, who doesn't even notice him, trance-like in her efforts to not vomit.

"Follow me, then. Just, ah, keep to the path. Don't stray from the path."

Gretchen rounds a corner ahead. Harry follows. Another movement to Lorene's left draws her attention. Small...child-sized, maybe? Just a big cat? A small dog? *Or a huge goddamn rat,* Lorene chuckles to herself as she rounds the corner. She stops at the mouth of what seems to be a long, smoky hallway, no sign of Harry or Gretchen in the short distance she can see ahead of her. Reaching through the smoke, pressing ahead, it grows thicker. Wraps around her in thick tentacles.

"Harry? Mrs. Marsh?"

Her feet are less visible, less defined. She begins feeling her steps rather than seeing them. The floor beneath her changes. She stops as she realizes she is off the path and...in a room?

"Uhh...Harry? Hello? Anyone? How far away can you possibly be?" Lorene calls. Movement in the smoke and the stacks of adult diapers all around her. "Hello? If this is another trick, Ypsilanti, I'm through. You might as well give yourself up right now." Nothing. The man seems stupid, but not so stupid to keep up the charade if this was one. So then...

Noises. Whispered hissing, clicks of knives or talons. Wet muscle movement.

"Harry? I think there's someone in here." Lorene begins backing away from the shapes. There are now at least four or five distinct figures moving in the mist and shadows. Slowly coming closer, coalescing more into focus. Lorene turns and runs in what she can only hope is the direction she just came from, shrieking and claws behind her, rushing closer. Slime slapping concrete. Lorene turns another corner, ducks between two piles of baby doll parts and half-melted candles, and finds herself back on the path, smoke still surrounding her but thinning noticeably. The sounds still draw closer and closer.

A hand clasps her shoulder and she whirls around, punching toward Harry Ypsilanti's face, who ducks out of the way with surprising agility.

"Harry!"

"Yeah, yeah, it's me. Watch the right hook there, Joe Louis. I heard ya screamin and was just comin to save ya… Looks like ya saved yerself. Really proves what Simone De Beauvoir says about women, huh?"

"What? Did you see…?"

"See what, kid?"

"…Nothing. Where the hell are we? How can this hallway be so big?"

"Beats me on the last one, kid, but we're almost there, the bedroom's just up ahead. Follow me, and keep close."

"All right. Do you really think we'll find anything in the bedroom?"

"Oh hell no, not if it looks anything like the resta this place. But I want to see the place a person like this sleeps! I can't even picture it, y'know? I wish they made a television or radio show about that…film or describe the inside a houses like these… *Trash Stackers*, you could call it…"

Once inside the bedroom, the smoke oddly dissipates. The room is in a similar state to the rest of the house, with piles of items, a box full of various colors of toothbrushes, plastic cups, and half-burnt matchbooks adorned with a variety of words and tiny images. Yarn in piles across the room, draped like cobwebs across furniture and lamps. Two teetering, festering piles of summer sausage rolls, all in various states of breakdown. A mountain of old Spam tins, long past expired, Lorene realizes is slowly pulsing.

"Please, Mr. Yaksolipso, I can't take another loss…what with my Snookie-kins running off last month…"

"It's…uh…" Harry begins, looking around at the piles of old TV antennae, and various Christmas ornaments everywhere, the stacks of syrupy baseball cards dripping strands of mucous-thickened spit. "It's Yp-sil-an-ti, ma'am. And that's just awful."

Lorene tries to move away a bale of yellow rubber gloves bound in a mass, which quivers but doesn't give, and instead pushes back on Lorene. She slips and falls into the flailing rubber, collapsing with it onto the bed, and pushing a large pile of empty cigarette packs off one side and onto the floor. Small flies scatter into the air like a cloud of sawdust.

On the bed, covered in mouse-bitten blankets, lies a frail-looking man in his late fifties or early sixties. He stirs and opens his eyes.

"Phillip!" Gretchen yells, rushing toward him and almost knocking Harry into a group of old wicker baskets, blackened around their weaves.

"What the hell is going on here, Gretchen?! Who are these people in our bedroom?" Phillip asks, sitting up.

"Well, I...I thought you was...lost or something. I didn't think you come home after work last night... So I called a, uh, private investigator."

"You what?! You hired a private dick to come find me sleeping in my own bed?!"

"Well, at least I knew not to call the police..."

"Ya dummy! Ya didn't pay him too, did ya?!"

"Well, I will have to ask for a small, uh, nominal consultation fee...for the time we spent here and everything, you know, helping...and for my associate here, you know, actually uncoverin you and everything," Harry says almost bashfully. Lorene can't tell if it is a ruse or if he's actually ashamed to have to ask for the fee.

Phillip storms out of the room, and Gretchen grabs a handbag from a pile of too many others to count.

"Well, thank you again. I couldn't take another shock, after my Snookie Snooks running away and all..." Gretchen stops herself. Clutching at her mouth with an old, stained scrap of cloth. She hands Harry a $100 bill and begins out of the bedroom. "Let's stay on the path this time!"

Harry stuffs the bill in his pocket and motions for Gretchen to lead the way. Just before they exit, in the last blackened, unidentifiable pile by the door, Lorene spots something different, something familiar jutting from the mound of garbled geometry. It is white, and appears to be covered in a soft fur, clumping now with beads of brown and amber semi-liquids.

"Harry," Lorene says, pointing.

"Oh no, kid... I hope that's not..."

"...Snookie-kins?"

"Damn it all to heck and back, we can't just not check now," Harry says gruffly, taking the bottom of his coat in his hand and reaching for the thin furry shape. Harry gives it a soft tug, and the body of a small white Maltese rolls out of the garbage toward them. Lorene squeaks and jumps back out of the way as the animal flops and rolls. Time stands still for a moment as she locks eyes with the dead animal, cold and glassy. Time begins anew and the carcass collapses, exploding outward, sending a wash of putrid insides, coagulated blood, and various types of insects across the floor. Lorene doubles over above it all, unable to hold in the retching long enough to even turn away from the goopy mess.

"Well, shit. I think we found Snookie-kins."

* * *

The inside of Harry's car seems clean after everything they've just seen, and Lorene is finally regaining control of her stomach. She presses her face against the warm glass as Harry starts the car back toward town.

More silence, occasionally broken by Harry drumming his fingers in rhythmless pattering, humming almost-imperceptible lines to unrecognizable tunes. Through the outskirts of Forest Rapids, faces outside the car lost to late August heat, blurry and hazy. Hidden by the fumes of the other vehicles and the flashes of sunlight through the houses and tree branches.

Harry stops the car in front of another home. Perfectly coiffed lawn. White paint on the fences like dried cliché.

"Okay, kid, case number two. Don't be scared or nothin, Harry Ypsilanti's here to protect ya."

"Thanks?" Lorene manages. She still has her doubts about this guy. He seems…kind of like a moron, really. Harry smiles at her and ducks out of the car. Lorene follows suit. She falls into step next to Harry as they make their way up the driveway.

"All right, so it sounds like we got ourselves a surveillance case next. I'm not really too sure about the details, lady wasn't so clear on everything on the phone, but we'll see what she's got for us." Harry raps his thick hand against the thin plywood front door.

* * *

Harry and Lorene pace the small backyard slowly. They are looking down, under the few objects around: the swinging bench, the woodpile by the garage. Looking for *something*.

"Big, tough Harry Ypsilanti, swayed by an old woman's tears." Lorene smirks. She pokes under a yellowing, shriveling hibiscus bush and finds only an old pair of gardening gloves.

"Yeah, yeah. Cute. She didn't say nothin bout no cats over the phone. Said she had a missing person, not a…critter."

"I thought you were a cat person anyway?"

"I am, I just don't want it gettin round town I do lost animal cases, or every Tina, Esmerelda, and Nansheng in the city will be callin me up."

Lorene looks quizzically at Harry. Were there many Nanshengs in Forest Rapids? What a truly odd man.

A soft mewing stops both instantly.

"Ah, you hear that?" Harry looks around. Another shrill little mew, force of kitty lungs and tiny mouth pried wide, tiny scratchy pop. "No way…"

Harry walks toward the fence, looking up into the ancient oak tree in the neighbor's yard, just out of reach of the fence.

"You think he's up there?" Lorene asks, joining him below the towering plant.

"I dunno…that's a good, what, seven, eight-foot jump, just to get there from the fence, right? It'd be tough—"

Another mew cuts Harry off mid-sentence. He looks up into the old, knotted plant.

"That's it, then. He's stuck in a tree. Swell." Harry looks to Lorene expectantly. She frowns.

"Why are you looking at me like that?"

"Look, kid, I like climbin trees as much as the next man-child, but I hurt my back the other day on the crapper, and, you know…"

"Ew. Fine." Lorene sighs heavily. At least it's a job, she thinks, not the first time today.

"Thanks, kid."

Halfway up the tree, Lorene spots the cat, clutching a branch and staring wide-eyed down at her.

"You look like a real private eye now, kid. And you thought this shit was all lightin dames' cigarettes, long coattails flapping in the shadows of night, gun-metal gleaming down moonlit alleys… Femme fatales and fisticuffs… This is the bare bones cold hard truth a the job, kid. It's mostly stuff like this, you know? I ain't no femme fatale, kid, least not that I know about."

Lorene has been mostly ignoring Harry as she sits in an open spot in the tree, a vantage looking out over the city. Afternoon sun draped with silk clouds waving past, soap suds in a cooling bathtub. Lorene notices a group of people a few blocks over, outside Gill's Electronics. They stand in a tense cluster while one of them unloads crates from a large, unmarked freight van. *What the hell is going on there?* Lorene adjusts for a better view. Two of the gathered men are arguing heatedly, but Lorene can't make out what they are saying. One of the men looks frightened. The yelling man steps forward, and pulls what appears to be a rubber chicken, yellow and floppy, from his jacket pocket and waves it in the other man's face. He raises the dangling prop and slaps the frightened man across the face with it, then places it back into his jacket. Two other men grab the frightened man, now silent and shocked looking, by the arms. They begin dragging him inside the building.

"All right, kid, Tarzan time's over! Grab the cat and get your ass back down to Earth, it's almost closin time!" Harry shouts up at her, jarring her from her thoughts and the altercation in the distance. When she looks up again, the men are all dispersing, fading into the growing shadows and brickface of the building.

"Oh, uh, okay. Almost there." Lorene ascends the final few branches and reaches the cat, who looks scared and helpless. "Oh, it's all right, little man. You'll be just fine, just let me—"

As soon as Lorene gets her arm around the shaking feline, it begins yowling and thrashing, trying to whip itself from her grasp. Sticks claws into Lorene's arm, teeth, kicks repeatedly with his back legs, digging into the soft flesh of her under-arm like Play-Doh. She calls out in pain and shock, and begins slowly descending the tree, one-armed, cat still convulsing and slashing the entire way down.

"C'mon, you only gotta get a little closer, then you can drop him. That's good, kid, you're doing good! Just a flesh wound, right? Walk it off when you get back down, you'll be fine."

* * *

The bus' window is slippery and warm against her face, but Lorene can't seem to find the energy to move it. She adjusts the bandage she holds on her arm, thinking it's stopped bleeding finally until a dark splotch begins spreading across the white fabric. Outside the window, kids run through a spurting fire hydrant, a gaggle of old men on a porch puff from little wood pipes, leering as the bus passes. Lorene turns away. A young boy in the seat across the aisle from her is staring at her. Lorene forces a weak smile, and the child spits a dark green slime onto the bus floor.

3

HARRY YPSILANTI STANDS at the entryway to Lorene's apartment, shaking his head as if trying to wipe away cobwebs or an attack by unseen particles in the air. He presses a large finger onto the buzzer, and Lorene answers from the window, dressed and looking refreshed. Harry smiles feebly up at her.

"So…is this what time we start? I thought you'd be here 'bright and early' like you said." Lorene cracks a smile back at him.

"Hell, this is early. You ain't never gonna see my face before ten o'clock any day of the week, unless I ain't gone ta bed yet. Even this bein up before noon shit…it ain't gonna happen too often. Late nights, though, if you want em. I'm a nightbird myself, I get all my best thinkin done at night."

"Good to know." So maybe that's when he's actually intelligible? "Would you like any coffee or anything?"

"No thanks, kid. We should probably get a movin. We got a busy day ahead of us."

"More cats and garbage?"

"Naw, we got a couple legit cases today, kid. Hope you're ready for it. I think you are."

"Okay, I'll be right down."

Late summer light filters in through the car's windows, warming the seats, the air, all the parts of Lorene's body. The trash in the backseat. She can smell sweat, and garbage, and…something else. Lingering basement funk.

"So we're lookin fer a guy name a Earl…Earl Sleschinger. He's been skippin out on his child support. I dunno, I picked this one up from my informant down at the police station. Somethin about them havin a hard time identifyin the creep or somethin, I dunno. We just gotta ID him, and maybe try to talk him inta turnin himself in."

"And if he doesn't want to turn himself in?"

"Well…we bust his chops and bring him in ourselves."

"This isn't detective work, this is bounty hunting."

"Look, kid, you got a lot to learn about this business. I been doin this fer almost twenty years, and my pops did it his whole life fore that. There's all kinds of parts to this job…any of em don't suit you, maybe you need to find somewhere else to be."

"I guess it's better than pulling cats out of trees…"

"You got ups and you got downs with this line a work, kid, just like anything. On the plus side, there's a nice reward for information leading to this scum-sucker's arrest. That don't hurt, right?"

"I guess not. So we're off to find a deadbeat?"

* * *

Harry eases the car to a stop in front of the town's auto salvage yard. A large dour-looking man stands rubbing grease slowly and lustily up and down the metal shaft of some unidentifiable car part.

"Okay, so I'm gonna have you sit in the car on this one. Apparently this asshole got a history of female trouble. Might be easier to talk to this shitbird man-to-man, no women folk around."

Lorene scowls at this but nods in the affirmative. Harry steps out of the car and into the warm afternoon air. Hit immediately by the smell of oil and charred rubber and concrete soaked with various chemicals. *I still can't tell if this guy is an actual idiot, or if he's just putting me on,* Lorene thinks. She watches Harry as he walks toward the shop. The man stroking the car part continues what he's doing, staring unblinkingly at Harry's approach. His coveralls say *Earl* in big white print, large enough for Lorene to read from her vantage point in the car.

"Howdy, friend. You Earl? Earl Schleshinger?" Harry asks, friendly, slowing the drawl of his voice a little more than normal.

"Nope."

"Huh. Well, the reason I ask, friend, is that…you know, your coveralls kinda have *Earl* printed on em there. And I'm kinda here, right now, lookin fer a guy named Earl. And you tellin me you ain't Earl…but the coveralls…so you can see where it's not addin up in my head, right?"

"Maybe it is. Maybe it ain't. Don't matter."

"Oh, uh…huh."

"Uh-huh."

"It's just that, it does matter, at least to me. And my client, Miss Holly Tanover."

The man stares at Harry. The hungover private investigator looks him over again, and sighs heavily. Earl bends over and retrieves a glass bottle from the ground. Harry's body tenses, trying to picture the flight path of the empty beer, if this brute does actually chuck it his way.

In one smooth arc he brings the bottle to his own face, smashing it into an opaque-brown confetti, shards tinkling dully as they hit the pavement below. Harry stares open-mouthed as Earl smiles, blood beginning to run down his face in little red licorice ropes. His eyes never leave Harry's. The stout detective spreads his legs a little wider, preparing to run if he has to. *Please don't make me chase you, pal…*

"Uh…yeah, I guess I'm here to… You, uh, got some…you got somethin on yer face, buddy…"

Earl reaches up and feels around his bleeding face. His fingers trace the shape of one of the larger pieces of glass protruding from his scalp and, without flinching, still staring full-bore into Harry's soul, he pulls it free from its skin-sheath. More blood runs down his face, dribbling off his chin and down his neck, sopping into the grey-blue of his uniform.

"Everything going okay, Harry?" Lorene calls from the car.

"Yeah—yeah, just peachy, kid. Just sit tight," Harry says. Earl's smile broadens as he cranes his neck to look toward Lorene, now in the driver's seat of Harry's car, her arm and head hanging out the window impatiently.

"Swell, Earl… Mr. Schlesinger. I came here to…uh, to tell you that Miss Holly Tanover has filed a report with the police that you haven't been paying child support for the sextuplets you sired with her, and, uh…huh… The blood just keeps comin, don't it?" Harry looks at the gushing cuts with amazement. "Uh…anyway, seems the local fuzz ain't been able to properly identify ya, can't imagine why, so…"

"The cops try. I make em hurt."

"You 'make em hurt'? Huh. That's fucked up, is what that is. You sound like a goddamn serial killer, fer chrissakes."

Earl opens his mouth and bares his yellowed teeth. "You gonna run away now."

"Goddamn it, Earl, I wish I could."

"Too bad for you." Earl narrows his eyes at Harry, which forces a fresh crimson dribble to spurt forth down his pocked forehead, over his brow, down, down.

"Anyway, you gotta start payin for those kiddos, Earl. Bein' a deadbeat dad ain't kosher here in Forest Rapids."

"You gonna make me?"

Harry sighs. He looks back at Lorene, who raises her arms questioningly. Harry looks Earl up and down, scanning for possible vulnerabilities. "I guess I'm gonna hafta, huh?" Harry cracks his knuckles. "Unless, of course, you wanted to come quietly—"

Harry lunges at Earl before he finishes his sentence, hoping the element of surprise will be enough to skew the fight in his favor. His right fist lands squarely on Earl's jaw, connecting with the full force of Harry's considerable weight and fighting experience. In a flash Earl counters Harry's punch with his own, in Harry's pudgy midsection, dropping the older man instantly. Harry coughs, chokes for a moment. He stands back up, legs vibrating. In fact, everything's vibrating. The whole world is, so much he's almost seeing double. Harry shakes his head and looks at Earl.

"You make funny noises. I let you run. Goodbye, nosy man," Earl says, crossing his arms. Harry reaches into his jacket for his pistol, and remembers it's in the car with Lorene as he fingers the empty shoulder holster. *Good job, Harry, you fuckin dipshit, rookie fuckin mistake goin on a job without your piece, you fuckin idiot... You might as well just go join ol Dickie boy's squad a meter readers and brain-dead psychopaths.*

"Look, pal, it don't gotta be like this. I'm just here tryna get ya ta do right by your kids and their momma. Ain't no need for this gettin physical nonsense."

"Okay, you had chance. Now we play." Earl begins rolling up his grease-stained sleeves. Muscles spill from the fabric. Harry readies himself, not the first time he's been pretty certain he'll lose. First time in front of a new partner, but... You ain't an old fogy yet, Harry Ypsilanti, there's still plenty a milestones left to look forward to. Well, just let it be over with quick. Hopefully this new kid has the good sense to jump on the radio and call the cop shop...not that those morons will do much good. Might help keep this colossus from turning me into a puddle, though... Please, just don't let this ape-shit bastard kill me. Not *here*. Not *this* asshole.

Earl steps toward Harry. Harry raises his fists, determined to go down swinging. *At least I'll get the first punch. I gotta be quicker than this sack of shit...*

Harry finishes this thought, and is on the cusp of beginning the next one, the one setting the parts of his body into the motion needed to field a punch, when Earl's fist ricochets off his face, almost through it. Harry can see and think only of the explosion of light, the sharpness of lightning running through his nose, up his temple, wrapping the curves of his eyeballs. And then the incredible darkness afterward.

4

HARRY COMES TO in a rush and a loud belch, and finds Lorene wrapped tightly around Earl, arm pulled up under his chin, his face reddening, his arms flailing wildly. He goes limp and Lorene drops him. Her fists begin striking the soft flesh of Earl's face and Harry feels as though his body is moving too slowly, held back by invisible, tiny grasping hands. He reaches Lorene and pulls her off the unconscious man.

"Kid! Kid! Don't kill him now!" he coughs, feeling and tasting the drying blood still draining down the back of his throat.

Earl lies battered and unconscious on the pavement. Lorene is still breathing heavily, sporadic shudders, blood on her knuckles and the sleeves of her shirt.

"Holy shit. You really did a number on this stupid shitkicker, didn't you? Hot damn, kid."

Sirens in the distance. Lorene snaps out of whatever trance or rut she is in, stillness passing over her. She looks to Harry expectantly.

"Don't worry about it, kid, we got this. Though, when the cops ask, just, uh, tell em I just happened by, after the fact, and stopped to see if you needed any assistance. Not too many people know the details about our friend over here, and if they find out I know, my informant in the department might be smoked out. So tell em whatever you gotta, just pretend as though you don't know me. I was just passin by, copacetic?"

"Uh-huh." Lorene steadies herself as the police cruiser rolls to a stop behind her, breath returning to normal, sweat at the edge of her scalp, along her tensing and un-tensing neck.

"All right, just what in the hell is going on here?! Both of you, freeze! All three of you! Oh God damn it, not you, Ypso...Yopsi...you asshole gumshoe!"

* * *

Lorene could tell this dipshit didn't believe a word she said. He kept looking at Harry and shaking his head slowly in disbelief as he wrote down Lorene's statement. At least he didn't seem to recognize her from her time on the force.

"So, this man…tried to jump you…out of the blue? You just happened to be walking around this part of town? Alone?"

"Yes, I was jogging," Lorene says tersely.

"Okay…and then…this happened? I mean—you did this?" The cop looks suspiciously between Lorene and the bloodied man on the ground.

"That's right. This homeless man just happened by, after I'd already secured the perp, and offered assistance."

"Hey, wait a sec, I ain't homeless—uh, yeah, that's right…just like I told ya. I was just happenin by, takin my mid-afternoon stroll. You boys ain't got nothin on me. I just stopped by to see if I could help. Just bein a good samaritan, ya know?"

"Goddammit, Harry, cut the crap! You're telling me this honey-drop monkey-stomped that slab of mountain over there into the bloody bits staining up the gravel?" the cop screeches at Harry.

"Well, I only saw the end of the altercation, but—"

"Shut yer trap, PI! I would try to get that monster's statement, but somebody did a number on his face and broke his jaw in at least a few different places. And I'm supposed to believe it was the young woman standing here in front of me, and not the grizzled, dope-smoking, former airborne infantryman…"

"I did warn him, Officer, that if he did not back off, I would use lethal force. He did not comply, and I was in fear of my life," Lorene says in a flat, steady voice.

"Uh-huh."

"And look at those knuckles, those er fightin wounds if I ever saw em," Harry says, pointing to Lorene's bloodied hands.

"Yeah, what about your face, pal? You gonna tell me you did that shaving or something?" The cop scowls at the bruises growing darker and puffier on Harry's face.

"Naw, I had ta give my cat a bath this mornin. He wasn't the most accomadatin about it."

"Go home. Get the hell outta here, Ypsoula—"

"Ypsilanti," Harry interrupts politely.

"—the fuck ever, PI! I even get a whiff of your godawful cologne anywhere on these streets again tonight, I'm taking you in for vagrancy, you understand me?" The cop looks sternly at Harry. Harry smiles and nods like they're just two old friends talking. "And you…"

The cop turns his attention back to Lorene, who crosses her arms and stares back at him.

"Try not to go looking in rough parts of town for trouble…do your jogging somewhere else. If you ask me, unofficially, if what you told me is true, you brought this on yourself. I've got your info…if I do get anything out of this psycho and it doesn't jive with even a single word of what you said, you're coming downtown." He puts his sunglasses on dramatically. "The coffee-shits fiasco was the last straw, Ypsil…Yesil…Yeep—"

"Ypsilanti—"

"Fuck off!"

After a moment, "But what about the reward?" The cop doesn't respond to Harry's call.

"Did he just say 'coffee-shits fiasco'?" Lorene asks, her features pinched halfway between confusion and amusement.

"Yeah, he did. C'mon, kid, let me buy you a milkshake. Or a whiskey sour."

* * *

The car ride's like slow motion. Like stuck in syrup. Like this afternoon is somewhere in a dream. Heat and still wind. Outside the window, Lorene sees abstractions of suburban life, mowers chewing across lawns with no drivers, rocking chairs rocking empty on porches, cars without hands clutching the wheel, without feet pressing the gas forward. All the signs of life without the life. Lorene can't seem to see any people, and she can't tell why. Is it in her head? Is there something happening out there? Along the edge of the old railroad tracks, no trains run here anymore, grass and weeds poking up between the rusty iron bars and moldering wooden slats. A face pokes up from the tall grass, watching them pass. Eyes pop and stare. She blinks, and they're still there as the car drives past.

"Is this…normal? Everything looks…" She trails off. How to finish that sentence? Everything looks deranged? That plain and simple?

"These are the dog days a summer, kid. This is when all the nutters come out. *Boil over* is more like it. And all the normies turn ta nutters. This is our busy season. This and Good Friday. That's why I hired you," Harry says quietly, as if worried someone on the street will hear him.

"So far it kinda seems like we've just been cleaning up the things the cops don't want to deal with," Lorene says flatly. She's too hot and too tired to try to keep her tone professional. To push the annoyance out of her voice.

"Oh, you betcha. That's a percentage of our business. Ain't my first choice, but in case you didn't notice, this ain't that big of a town. Gotta get the work where we can. Besides, I got my ways of gettin even. Passive aggressive, y'know?" Harry grins. They turn a corner to find the warped, scraggly outlines of three dogs mounting each other. Lorene's mouth literally drops open without her even noticing, her eyes stuck to the trio as they pass. One of the dogs, a basset hound, looks at Lorene as they pass and bares its teeth. It takes her a moment to come back from the sight.

"So…like the 'coffee-shits fiasco'?" she asks.

Harry's smile grows. "Yeah…maybe. And some other things. I'll show ya. Reach behind yer seat there, and grab that little black bag. Yup. Now open it up, there should be a bottle…should be marked *Industrial Grade Laxatives*."

Lorene pulls the bottle of pills from the leather satchel. She looks them over. Harry keeps looking over at her expectantly, grinning.

"And?"

"And? The fuck you mean, 'and'? Laxatives, kid, they make ya shi—"

"Yeah, I know what they do. But that's it? Just give them some laxatives and watch them run to the can en masse?"

"Well, yeah. I mean, not quite. I left right quick after I dumped it in their coffee pot. I just sorta…imagined it."

"You didn't even stay to watch? I'm disappointed in you, Mr. Ypsilanti."

"Hey, you got somethin better, kid, let me hear it."

"Okay. Give me a little time. I'll give you something." Lorene gives a conspiratorial grin.

"All right, you think on it. Right now, we need to try to get that reward money for our friend Earl. C'mon, let's go see if we can make these coppers pay up."

"I don't think they're going to give us anything. We didn't physically bring him in…"

"Yeah, but those shit-burgers wouldn't of been able to get him in custody if it wasn't fer us. Me distractin him by lettin him use my face as a punchin bag, you by beatin the ever-lovin tar outta him. You ain't heard Harry put on the old smooth-talkin routine. I can be pretty convincin once I get warmed up. Just let me do the yappin, and agree to anything I say, okay?"

"Huh?"

"I mean, like, play along, kid. If I tell any fibs. I'm not havin ya sign yer soul over to tha Devil or nothin."

* * *

In through those familiar double doors. Solid metal sliding stiffly back into place behind them. The uneven step up into the lobby. The way the light sweeps across the old plaques hung on the walls. The lobby smells like stale testicles, gunmetal, and burnt coffee. Lorene stops to look at a new picture hung on the wall. Harry nods toward it.

"What is it, kid? Someone you know?"

"Yeah…me. That's my arm, right there. I got cropped out. They took this the day they let me go, right after the big welcome home party for the boys."

"That's cold-blooded. At least they let ya stay for the party before they shit-canned ya."

The officer behind the front desk had been standing silently watching them from the moment they entered. He clears his throat impatiently.

"Hey there, Jackie, my man!" Harry calls jovially.

"It's Officer Warner. What the hell do you want, Yippiedonkus?"

"Ol Dickie Boy in? Me and him gotta talk business."

"Chief Smith isn't in right now, PI."

"Look, just let me in to see him right quick, I'll only take five minutes of his time, then he can go back to strokin his pistol and I can get out yer hair."

"He isn't here, you chicken-fucking—"

"Whoa, whoa, now. No need for that sorta language around a lady. We'll let you get back to pickin on teenagers and syphonin jelly outta donuts. We'll check back later."

"Get the hell outta this station, Yapsalando!"

"Ypsilanti, boy-o. Get it right next time." Harry turns and glares at the young officer sharply, and the man's features drop, fear glinting across his eyes for a moment. Harry begins back through the metal doors, and Lorene glances once more at the group picture on the wall before she follows him outside.

Being back inside the stationhouse made Lorene queasy. She didn't think Officer Warner had recognized her; he was too busy sparring with Harry, and she had only met him once or twice. She'll have to get used to it, she guesses—it seems like they'd be interacting with the local constables more often than she would have liked. It'll get easier. It has to…right?

✳✳✳

"So…that went…something," Lorene says, trying to wipe away another of these awkward silences that she's beginning to suspect is only awkward on · her end.

"Yeah. You ever smoke ganja before?"

"What?"

"Ganja, cannabis, tea, the viper, the devil's weed. You ever try it?"

"You mean marijuana?"

"I mean you ever smoke it before? Even just once?"

"Uh…no." Lorene looks at Harry to try to deduce if this is another test of some sort. Sure, she's heard of reefer. Sure, she's curious. But she's never tried it.

"Never? Not even once out of curiosity?"

"Nope."

"Wats da madder whiff you kid, you a tee-totaler or somethin?"

"No, it's just… It's illegal. And dangerous. I've seen the documentaries about it. Besides, I wouldn't even know where to get it if I did want to try it," Lorene says, a bit hurt at being read as quite so conservative. She's had her moments. Nights spent riding in cars with boys, drag racing on the nearly empty streets as if they owned them. That time in high school she and a friend had shoplifted a bottle of brandy from the local grocery store. Nothing *that* crazy, but… She's no nun, that's certain.

Harry sticks a long, thick cigarette between his lips and flicks open a metal lighter engraved with the words *Wake Up and Fight!*

"Are you going to be all right to drive?" Lorene asks, eyeing the joint as he lights it.

"Huh? Oh, this? Shit, this is like my morning coffee, y'know? Quick pick me up, nothin more. Are you sure I can't interest you in a small taste? It's really not like those dumbass movies make it out to be. Reefer madness my armpit… Worst thing it ever done to me is put me to sleep."

The smell drifts to Lorene, spicy and green like fresh vegetables, incense, and farmers markets. It smells like something she would want to eat, a spice for salad or some exotic pastry. It licks at the small curves of her nose, rolls dryly across her eyes. The only other place she'd encountered the drug was in the evidence locker downtown, among the confiscated guns and swords, the box of dynamite, the human skin stretched into a dagger-sheath they'd pulled from some loony drifter they had found wandering the street one night, tucked away next to the two German hand grenades some kid had found washed up on the beach just after the war ended. "I don't know. It's illegal…"

"So's what ya did to Earl's face yesterday, technically, but who am I to judge? Hey, kid, I have it on pretty good authority your boss won't mind."

"I guess, if you think it's okay." Lorene takes the smoking tube from Harry.

"Just take a little puff, like a cigarette. You ever smoked a cigarette, kid?"

Lorene just glares at Harry and takes a long draw from the joint. She begins choking and lurching, almost dropping the joint as she hands it back to Harry, unable to compose herself.

Oh Jesus, what did I just do?

"You'll be all right, just cough it out, cough it out. You need some water or somethin, kid?"

Lorene stops shuddering and gasping, now just shakes slightly and wheezes. "No... I'll be all right."

Through the window, Lorene finds a world unlike any she's ever known. Harry begins flipping through stations on the radio. Outside, a haze at the edges of vision, people popping from colors and beams of light. All their faces are too funny. Lorene giggles. Tries not to. Giggles more. Harry flips radio stations, only stopping for a second or two before continuing ahead. Outside the car, individual water droplets land on individual blades of grass. Puppies bark and their voices don't sound for a moment, like thunder's lazy response to lightning. Outside the car, the city laughs. Laughs at Lorene, peers in at her; it *knows* what she's doing, what she's on. It knows the state she's in. Outside the car, two men are unloading a large, strange vat of chemicals from a van into the back dock of the movie theater. Odd faces, more than just this fuzzy blanket laid across Lorene's brain, the one she has to poke through to see anything. These men are more strange than Lorene is high, she is sure of it. Bad eyes, shifty bodies. They keep looking around like guilty kids. Like villains in movies, up to no good. The serials before full-length movies. Evil henchmen or maniacal Martians. The crates say *Forest Rapids Meat Packing Plant*, and it takes Lorene a moment to realize why this is odd.

"They don't serve meat at the movie theater, do they?!" Lorene blurts suddenly, aware it's too loud as it's escaping her mouth. Harry jumps a little in his seat.

"Huh? Oh, no, I guess not. They used to have frankfurters, but the machine broke. Why, you hungry kid? We can stop over at Big Tom's Diner if you want a bite ta eat real quick. Sometimes this stuff, it makes ya a bit peckish, to put it mildly. You know me, I'm always up for wastin time on the company dime."

"I...I'm not hungry," Lorene manages.

"I hear ya, kid... Ya doin okay?"

"Uh-huh... I think so. Probably. Am I doing okay?"

Harry chuckles. "Yeah, yer doin just fine. You'll come down in about an hour or so. For now, just enjoy the ride..."

5

LORENE'S HEAD FEELS like it's stuffed full of old newspapers. Everything is crowded, and padded, and inky. She hears all the voices on the page like her conscience talking in different tongues, at different volumes. Everything seems scrambled. And yet, she is slowly getting used to it. She is learning how to make her mouth move in all this jelly. Her arms and legs. Like learning to compensate for limbs pushing through water, but thicker—clear mud.

She stares down at the files Harry had spread out on the table before her. She tries to read the words on one of them and quickly gives up. As good as hieroglyphics, strange symbols wrap and tangle the page. A cigarette hangs from Harry's dry lip, unlit. His eyes are red and glassy, and he is lost in the paper in his hand.

"You ever hear about this Freck guy? Chandler Aloucious Freck…"

Lorene shakes her head in the negative.

"Seems the police has had…more'n a few dealings with this upstandin citizen. First, they caught him creepin around town outside women's windows, wearin a tin-foil suit—"

"Eww."

"Uh-huh. Trust me, it gets better. Caught gambling and playing five-card stud with Mrs. Farble's kindergarten class…using heroin…trying to sell heroin to Mrs. Farble's kindergarten class…attempted sodomy of the mayor's dog, Snickerdoodle… Lewd thoughts."

"Lewd thoughts?" Lorene looks at Harry suspiciously.

"Yah, one a those batshit bonkers laws still on the books here. Pretty much never enforced. Only like three people have ever been charged with it, and two of em were a priest and a nun runnin an 'anything goes' brothel around tha turn a tha century."

"But how can you even prove it?"

"I guess someone got a signed confession outta Freck. Prolly part a his plea deal for the bestiality and the drug charges. Guess who was fucking arresting officer in that shitshow of a case? Our own future Chief-O, Dick Smith himself. After that case, he got himself promoted. Moved up the ladder right quick. Now he's Chief of Police Richard Smith…Old Dickie Boy, as me, and probably his momma, affectionately call him."

Lorene scowls. "That asshole."

"Uh-huh. *That* asshole. The hard-ass of all hard-asses, the bully of all bullies. You probably didn't work with him much, did ya? He was over there, with us, during the war…although that little weasel just copped a cushy desk job as some general's fuckin coffee boy or somethin. He didn't even see any fightin. Guy's a prick, plain and simple, and just about everyone in town is on the same page with me on that, even his own coppers. Smith's up to some shady shit, you mark my words. But I never catch him doing anything illegal…he doesn't even drive over the speed limit."

"I know him a little bit. He *is* an asshole…but maybe you can't catch him doing anything because he isn't doing anything. He is the chief of police, after all."

"No way. He's too clean. Even for a chief of police. That rat bastard's up to something, believe you me. Anyway, like I said, this Freck guy's got a rap sheet that would curl a sailor's toes. He's a verified racist, been caught hassslin or hurtin minorities on more'n one occasion…he's onea them West Forest Rapids Baptists too, those pieces of fuckin work. He must have some kind of connection in the department or a really good lawyer or somethin, cause most of the time he gets away pretty much free and clear."

Even with all four fans running full blast and the window wide open, the little office is an oven, broiling Lorene's outsides, her insides basted with cannabis and reservations. Bad vibes. For about the tenth time in the last couple of days, Lorene wonders if she has made a mistake taking this job.

"My source down at the station says they issued a warrant for this guy for runnin a model airplane glue sniffing ring, but they were told not to act on it yet. So I say, let's get there before they change their minds, and take him in ourselves…hopefully collect the standard bounty on him, at least. Hell, maybe you'll even be able to beat the shit outta somebody again today!"

* * *

Freck's house is squat and battered, chipped blue paint outside, windows covered by yellow curtains. Sitting on a nearly empty street, an empty lot to both sides between Freck and his nearest neighbor, it looks like a pile of roadkill standing up with one last gasp of breath. Decked out with old tires as a flower garden, a pile of broken and disassembled lawnmowers as bushes and shrubbery up near the house. The front door is nearly closed, but isn't. Ajar an inch or so. Red flags in both their minds, Lorene and Harry unholster pistols at the same time.

"You thinkin what I'm thinkin?"

"Something doesn't look right?"

Harry nods. "Yep. Stay behind me, kid. Cover me at the doorway, I'll clear the corners." Harry moves swiftly, and the sudden tactical reasoning he is displaying surprises Lorene. Harry pushes the door open further, slowly.

"Hello, Chandler Freck? This is Harry Ypsilanti, I'm a private investiagto—"

A body swings down at Harry and he shrieks, high-pitched, piercing. He fires twice into it, spraying blood and flecks of Freck's flesh everywhere. "Aw, Jesus. I think we found our guy."

"Oh…God. What the hell happened?" Lorene stares at the hanging body as it slows its lurching, her pistol still trained on its midsection, blood draining in little red ropes of licorice out of the holes Harry just put in him.

"Looks like somebody stuck him good a couple times right in the chest, and strung him up here…while he was still alive. Look at these marks on the wall. And this blood, it's still soupy. This couldn't a happened that long ago."

Lorene manages to hold back the gagging, but tears stream from her eyes.

"Aw shit, c'mon, kid, let's get ya outta here. This ain't none'a our business now anyway." Harry wipes a chunk of gore from Lorene's shoulder and leads her gently back toward the car.

"Sorry you had to see that on your second day, but it comes with the territory, I guess. After you've seen enough of em… Ah, who'm I kiddin? It still don't get any easier to see, just easier ta forget. But, I mean, workin at tha cop shop, you prolly know how many homicides we get in this city."

"Actually, while everyone was off in the war we only had one homicide, and that was a woman who killed her draft-dodger husband who had been beating her for years."

"Huh. Well, you want anything? Shot a rum? Horse tranquilizer? More dope?"

"How about just a cigarette?"

"Sure, kid. Sure." Harry lights a cigarette for both of them. Quiet as the car rolls down the street. The sun seems to falter, it falls, it turns colors and spreads out thinly across the horizon line.

* * *

Outside of Lorene's apartment, Harry stops her.

"Hey, kid…"

Lorene looks at him, annoyance rolling briefly across her already exhausted face. What the hell else does he want? Harry smiles back dumb and unreadable.

"Take this." He tosses her the pack of cigarettes. "You relax tonight. Try to leave the job at the office, right? I know it's tough—Jesus, do I know. But just try to take it easy. Do somethin to take your mind offa things. I think *Captain Patriot* is on the TV tonight."

"Thanks, Harry. I'll see you tomorrow, huh?"

"Yeah? Yeah…I'll be here. My usual time."

* * *

Lorene paces for a long time after Harry drives away, chain smoking the pack of cigarettes and thinking through everything. She turns on the television, and *Captain Patriot* plays to the room without her noticing. She doesn't know why she was so affected; she hadn't known Freck, and from what Harry told her about him, she didn't want to. But the way he'd just been…shanked, and strung up like a pig being bled…it didn't sit well with her. "Just something else I'll have to get used to with this job," she says aloud, and instantly recants it. *Please, don't let that be something I get used to.* Dealing with a doper boss, the boys club down at the Forest Rapids PD, that shit she could get used to. Sadistic, EC comic-type murders…not really what she was looking for in a career direction.

She takes a final long draw from the half-smoked cigarette in her hand, looks at it with slight disgust, and flicks it out the window. She pulls the blinds.

On the street below, a man approaches the smoke as it hits the sidewalk in a small pop of red-orange embers. He picks it up and draws on it in a series of rapid breaths, his face dull, cold, smooth. Too smooth, as if he is wearing a Halloween mask or a layer of cellophane. He smokes as he walks toward a car parked on the street. Another man sits inside. Features blank, as if he is wearing a rubber mask as well. He turns the radio up: a broadcast about Freck's murder. The other man chuckles as he gets inside the car. He takes one final look up to Lorene's darkened window as the car drives away, shoving the lit cigarette into his mouth and chewing slowly, methodically. His rubber-faced smile never changes.

6

"SO, NOT TRYNNA pry or nothin, kid, but I gotta ask. You okay? I mean, if that was yer first…uh, you know…yesterday…" Harry doesn't take his eyes off the road, his voice as soft as Lorene has heard it. Almost parental. "I mean, the fuckin blood and shit an everythin, man, seein him hoisted up there like a fuckin rack a ribs… Goddamn." Almost.

"Yeah. Yeah, I'll be okay. At first I was, you know…a little shook up."

"Oh, Jesus turkey nuggets, that first one, it really sticks ya good, don't it? I remember my first one, it was—"

"But I think I'll get over it. It's just a body, right? I mean, it goes with the job, right?"

"That it does, kid…more often than I'd like. No middle ground in this gig. Either we're pullin cats outta trees or guts outta the soles of our shoes."

Lorene nods at this stoically.

"And there's a fine line between not lettin that shit get to ya, and never lettin anything get to ya… Ya lose yer humanity, fall too far over the line, you become one a them, kid. Those creeps out there, the ones we're supposed to be bustin up… That divide between us and them, kid, it ain't too wide. Ain't too wide at all."

"Surprisingly insightful, Harry." Lorene smirks.

"Yeah, every once in a while."

"Look, I think I'll be fine. Thanks. For, you know, giving me a shot and everything."

"Hey, I want you to know… You're a good fit here, kid. I like havin ya around. Yer gonna do great here, if you want to stay, that is."

"Thanks, Harry. So what's the first case today? Somebody lighting dog shit on fire on people's porches?"

"No, I actually solved that one earlier, on the way ta pick ya up. It was the person who called it in. Let's head to Big Tom's, grab some coffee, fuel up for the day, and I'll tell ya all about it. Big Tom's got tha best coffee in town, in my opinion."

"Isn't it the only place with coffee in town?" Lorene asks bemusedly.

"Well, that don't make it not tha best, do it?' Harry smiles back at her. "C'mon, kid, another day, another dollar."

* * *

Big Tom's Diner is just off Main Street, at the edge of the town center. A large open space, windows as walls the entire way around, a large linoleum-topped counter making an L in the center of the room, Big Tom's short frame bouncing nimbly behind it, pouring coffee, sliding plates of pie and eggs across it to the bodies pressed into the stools and each other all around it. Tom's sister, Trina, is taking an order from an elderly couple at one of the tables when Harry and Lorene enter.

"Hey, Harry, how are you this morning? Here for the usual?"

"Nah, just coffee today, T. Me and the new partner got a long day ahead a us, we gotta get out there quick as we can today."

"Well, just grab yourself a seat anywhere, I'll pop over to ya in a sec, hon."

Harry and Lorene take a seat near one of the windows.

"So, what's on the docket today, Mr. Ypsilanti?" Lorene asks, looking around at the group gathered around them. Old people slurping down breakfast and watching the cars go by, a scruffy-looking man sitting at the counter who looks like he may not have been to bed yet, a few others scattered around.

"Well, we got a couple things. I'm still a bit hung-up on the whole Freck thing. Somethin seems fishy about all that, kid. We're gonna keep pokin around that one, but we still gotta pay the bills, so we got a couple more of the banal ones too."

The little bell atop the diner's heavy metal door jingles quietly, and Harry looks up to see Clarence Krieger and Chief Smith shuffle in, looking at the other customers with disdainful glares. Smith's eyes meet Lorene's first, then Harry's. His lips purse into some kind of hideous parody of a smile. Animal mimicry. His short, thick frame saunters toward their table.

"Well, well. Harry Ypsidouchous, fancy finding you here just sittin around. I had heard you finally found someone else stupid enough to join your little Mickey Mouse club. So, are you fitting in better as a PI's secretary than a police officer's?" Smith grins cruelly.

Hatred like bile in the back of Lorene's throat. Heat and rage. Flashes of Smith's skull rushing up beneath Lorene's pulsing fists, red paint across the diner's scuffed tiles. Brains fly out in this dream, splattering the scrambled eggs of the little old man the next table over, mixing with the yellow cottonballs and the slabs of ham. Lorene clenches her teeth and looks directly up into Smith's small dark eyes. His gaze leaps from hers, terrified wood animal, back to Harry.

"Lorene here is my new partner, Dickie Boy. You really dropped the ball on that one, Chief-O, she's a solid crimebuster."

Smith scoffs, and Krieger behind him does as well, a noise between a donkey's braying and a man with a cube of cheese caught in his throat. "I heard you been sticking your nose in a lot of official police business lately, Yapsidoodle. Almost like you got some kind of line on the comings and goings of my department."

"Just got a nose for the dregs a society, I guess," Harry drawls back at him.

"Got your nose right up the ass of the dregs of society is more like it," Smith growls. Krieger guffaws again, head nodding dumbly.

"What the hell d'ya want, Smith? My partner and I are in a logistical meetin here, so if ya don't mind…"

"What do we have for today? Helping old ladies cross the street? More cats in trees? Somebody's kid need a spanking?" Smith smirks.

"What a pathetic wad of crap you are," Krieger croaks. Harry looks at him hard.

"Kids need a spankin. That's a good one, Dickie Boy. You got that Grade A wit, sure do. I guess that's why all'a your coppers are always sayin, 'Dick for Brains,' right? A term a endearment for their great leader?"

Smith steps toward Harry and looks as if he is about to strike him.

"Do it, Chief-O. Give me a reason ta defend myself. One free shot, that's what ya get."

Krieger and Lorene look at their bosses uncertainly, not sure if they should intervene or if they even can.

"I could beat the shit out of you right now, Ypsildookie, and then arrest you for assault on an officer for the damage you did to my fists, you hear me?! I'm the top dog in this town, you—you are just a flea on my balls. You read me?"

Harry stares up at Smith with a mixture of pity and bemusement. "You get that from a Bogie movie, Dickie Boy? Real scary line, it was. If you didn't ape that from a movie, Chief-O, I'm writing it down in my little notebook to use sometime."

Smith turns and swiftly exits the diner. Krieger looks at Harry and then Lorene with a smarmy gaze and follows his boss.

* * *

"That fuckin guy. Five fuckin minutes alone wit him, kid, five minutes…that'd be a mighty nice Christmas present."

"So… What next, Harry? What's our first case for today?"

"In a hurry to get ta work, are we? Okay, okay, here, first one. A Trisha Arnheim, fifteen, possible runaway, but the mother is gettin real worried about her and wants us ta look inta it. Last known location we have on her is at her home, after school two days ago. The mother is at work, but she told me she'd leave the back door unlocked so we can take a look around, see if there's anything we can find might give us a clue where she went."

***

At the back door of the Arnheim family home, Harry stops.

"Kid, I got a tingle in my medula oblongata…"

"Uhh…is that good or bad?"

"Not good, kid. Not today, at least."

"What do you want to do? Should we go in?"

"I dunno. Stay sharp, hear me? Let's see what we see."

Nothing in the house seems particularly out of place as Lorene and Harry move cautiously through it. They make their way to Trisha's room.

Harry nods at Lorene but doesn't say anything as he pushes the door open.

Inside they find the normal room of a fifteen-year-old girl. Yellowish-cream walls, floral wallpaper elements that match the bedspread. A single crucifix on the wall above the bed. Clean, sparse, nothing strange as they take an initial survey of the small room.

"What's that over there?" Harry asks, stepping toward the small dollhouse on the wall opposite the bed. He bends toward it, and Lorene leans in behind him. Harry wrenches up suddenly, bellowing garbled curses and spitting into the air.

"Harry!" Lorene screams, pulling her pistol and aiming at the dollhouse. "What happened?!"

"It's okay, it's fine… It's just my fucking back!" Harry grumbles and stands bolt straight, a sinewy crack emanating from his lower back as he does. "Goddamn, there it goes!"

"Jesus, Harry, don't do that. I thought something got you."

"Something? C'mon, kid, don't go letting your imagination run wild now, okay? We gotta stay sharp for our clients."

"Harry, what's that?" Lorene asks, pointing down at the dollhouse. Inside is what appears to be a small piece of paper, folded hastily. The paper appears to have some red stains dried along it. "Harry, maybe we should check it out."

"I know. I don't wanna, but...we should prolly check it out."
Harry reaches for the scrap of paper cautiously. Both detectives have their weapons drawn and trained on the dollhouse, tense, waiting, creeping closer, breath ragged and slow and almost forgotten. Harry reaches out and dislodges the paper, which comes loose with a burble of liquid and a horrific squelching noise. Slickness and grit. An almost neon fluorescence, green and brownish and streaked with strands of scarlet; more of the red splashes up around the edges of the paper as Harry pries it loose. Foamy and soft, Harry flicks the substance from his fingers and groans disgustedly.
"What is it, Harry?"
"I don't know, kid, you was a teenage girl before, not me. Is it, like, normal?"
"The fuck, Harry. No, green slime isn't normal teen girl stuff. What's that?"
Lorene points at the trail of goo, which has begun to dribble down the dollhouse and into a large chest beneath it.
"Not the chest. You don't think... Ew, this ain't gonna be pretty, kid. You should check it out."
"It says your name on the sign outside the office, Harry, not mine. This one is all yours."
Harry grunts and peers down at the dribbling trail of slime. He leans in, and in a quick motion topples the dollhouse, pulling up the top of the chest and revealing a mangled, almost porcelain-colored body inside, about the size of a child.
"Oh Jesus! What is it?!"
"Uh, Harry, I think it's just a doll."
"Oh, fuck me sideways, kid. I thought it was our missin teen or somethin, or some kinda undead creature from beyond the grave..."
"Harry, look at the note!" Lorene has picked up the sopping piece of paper and is unfolding it delicately. She holds it up for Harry to read as it drips more stringy burps of brownish slime.
"What is it? What's it say?"
"It just says, 'Find the Bodies.'"
"Find the bodies? The fuck does that mean? Is that some kind a youth slang I don't know about, like bumpin uglies or somethin?"
"Uh, I have no idea, Harry. Maybe it literally means *find the bodies*. Maybe it's a clue?"

"Maybe. Don't make much sense to me. I hate to do this, but...I think we better go talk to Dickie Boy."

"I don't want to go anywhere near those assholes, especially after that little run-in back at Big Tom's."

"I know, kid, but this feels like somethin bigger'n just a missing girl. From the looks a this place, I'm wondering if this all has somethin to do with our deceased from yesterday too. We gotta let the coppers know about this one. Professional courtesy and all. They may not send it our way, but I'll be damned if anyone can ever say I didn't try. And maybe we can still get that money for our buddy Earl too."

"Okay. Can we make a quick stop? I have to make a phone call."

"Phone call? Who da hell ya callin in tha middle a tha day?"

"It was my sister's birthday yesterday, and I already forgot to call her earlier. I don't want to be any later."

"Fine, we'll swing through the office, I can grab a couple more reefers while you make yer phone call."

* * *

Standing outside the police station, looking in at the full lobby. A banner stretches across the room with *Happy Birthday* printed in fading multi-colored letters. Officers are spread throughout, grouped in pairs or small clusters of three or four. A cake sits uncut on the processing desk. Lorene shifts the box of donuts in her hands and sighs heavily.

"You ready for this? You can wait in the car if you want, kid. I'd understand," Harry says, shoving part of a bearclaw into his mouth.

"No way. I'm ready."

"Okay. Great idea, by the way, about the donuts. Butter-up ol Chief-O, make him a bit more...agreeable."

* * *

"—You annoying little leech, Yapsolantics! Why are you even in my office right now?"

"Well, sir, it's about this case I'm on, uh, we're on—"

"Shut up, shut your stupid face. I told you, stop being a goddamn nuisance to me and my town, you hear me? Jesus, all the time I waste dealing with and thinking about your worthless ass—"

"Thanks, Chief. Gets me all warm and sloppy inside to hear you think about me so much."

"Shut up! And don't even get me started about your pranks! All the shit you've tried to pull!"

"Sir, if I may." Lorene speaks up for the first time, firmly but respectfully. "We've found a strange link between two cases we've recently been working on, the murder of Chandler Freck and the disappearance of—"

"Shut up! Both of you! I don't want to hear any of it! Get this dame outta my station, scumsucker, I got real police work that needs to get done! We don't have time for your sleazeball antics, Yapsidoinkle! Now go!"

"Hey, look, I was just tryna help, be a good samaratin, let you know—" Harry begins.

"Another word, biscuit dick, and I'll throw both of you in the drunk tank for the night, you hear me? Get gone! And leave the donuts!"

Harry looks like he is going to say something else, but scowls and storms out of the room. Lorene glares at Smith, who doesn't look directly at her, and tosses the box of donuts onto his desk.

In the lobby, all the officers are watching Harry and Lorene as they leave.

"What's the matter, PI, Cap'n take your donuts?" the cop who had taken Earl away calls from across the lobby. Harry gives the room the finger as the other officers shriek with laughter in unison. Lorene smiles at them coolly.

"Go on, gumshoe, and take this dizzy broad with you before she screws something up in here. This is a place for men's work," Krieger chimes in forcefully. He stares at Lorene as he says this. The two detectives leave. Outside in the sunlight, Lorene can see Harry shaking.

"Who da fuck does he think he is? We're comin in there, completely jovial, trynna share a professional tip, maybe help save some girl's life… What the hell are you smilin bout?" Harry crosses his arms and looks sternly at Lorene. She just continues smiling back at him, basking in his momentary helplessness. "That old fartbag back there insults us, insults *you*, and you just out here smirkin away…"

"I'm smiling because I came up with a better plan, Harry."

"A better plan a what? How ta get our Earl moolah? How ta talk ta that asshat back there?"

"The other day, you told me to come up with a better way of getting even with these jerks. I did. I came up with a really good plan, Harry. And it's already in motion." Lorene holds up the bottle of laxatives, unscrews the top as Harry looks on inquisitively, and upends it. Nothing comes out.

"Holy shit, kid, I think you just exploded my brain a little bit. So, what, ya dumped all the laxatives in their coffee or somethin? That's pretty intense. I didn't see you even do it."

"That's because I didn't dump them into the coffee, Harry. I put them in the donuts. Now, let's head back to the car and I'll tell you all about it. We should have the perfect vantage for the show from over there… We can see right in through the glass. See?" Lorene points, and Harry sees two of the officers inside making obscene gestures out at the pair. Krieger approaches the others with the box of donuts Lorene had left on the chief's desk. The cops descend on the box, scarfing down the pastries lewdly and slobbishly. Crumbs and gobs of frosting drop to the floor; a small spurt of jelly spatters across the bottom of the window. Tongues where they shouldn't be. Phallic connotations, more sexual gestures directed out toward the street.

"Jesus, that's disgustin. But how'd ya'know Dickie Boy wouldn't keep alla tha donuts for himself? Not that Chief-O shitting his brains out is necessarily a bad plan, but…" From the car, the pair are able to see into the station, but don't seem to be drawing the attention of the occupants any longer.

"Smith only eats the custard-filled ones, trust me. He made that very clear when he'd send me out to get coffee and donuts for the station."

"Yeesh. What a piece of work this guy is. Wait, kid, you let me eat one a them donuts!" Harry's face lights up red, his eyes widen. His mouth opens and closes quickly; Lorene thinks she can almost hear the rusty gears of his brain twisting and slapping behind his skull.

"Relax, Harry, I put it in after you took yours, so they would see you eating one and think it was safe. While you were talking to that squirrel when we first pulled up."

"Oh yeah, Brixton, we're pals now. I wondered why you didn't come introduce yourself to him," Harry says matter-of-factly. Lorene looks at Harry, wondering if he is joking or sincere. "Well, that sounds like a pretty great plan, kid. I mean, kind of derivative of mine, but, you know, it expands on it a little, I guess. I'm impressed."

"Harry Ypsilanti, I'm disappointed at how little imagination you have. I haven't even gotten started yet. So…slip em the laxatives. I like that part of your plan. It's a good, solid foundation. But I've gone a little further. First…" Lorene looks down at her wristwatch for a few long moments, waiting. Harry's breathing is heavy, loud in the near-silence, face pinched in wide-eyed anticipation, working his hands on the steering wheel and staring at Lorene.

"First what, kid, there's more? C'mon, I'm dyin over here!"

"First, we add a little extra chaos to the mix." Lorene looks up, and nods toward the station. A line of about twelve or thirteen Jehovah's Witnesses have approached and are entering the police station, single-file. They are all dressed in identical white dress shirts, pressed black dress pants, immaculate thin black ties.

"Okay…"

"I may have expressed some interest, on behalf of the guys at the station, of course, in the Good Word."

"Jaysus on the cross, I say."

"Next, we disable the toilets." Lorene can't contain herself any longer, and a grin cracks her face open.

"Okay. And how in the hell are we gonna go about that?"

"We did it already, Harry. Or, rather, I did it. One well-placed phone call to a local plumber, one Mr. Spuddle, happens to live across from me. Real nice fella. Also happens to have a mammoth grudge against Chief Smith and the *Law* in this town. It didn't take much sweet talk to get him to help. I simply offered to mow his lawn for the rest of the summer and he was in, no questions asked. I told him to take out the toilets whatever way he saw fit. Quick and quiet were the only stipulations."

"Keep goin, kid, I'm palpitatin here. Regular Orson Welles a devilish pranks, you are." Harry fans himself as Lorene continues.

"Well thank you. All right, so the station is flooded with bodies, chaos, complaints. The cops are frazzled and don't know how to even start sorting it all out when *Boom*—the, ahem, *call of nature* takes hold. It won't take long before they realize their bathrooms are useless and, hopefully, we get to watch the boys in blue waddle over to the elementary school here and try to commandeer their facilities." Lorene chuckles.

"And we got front row seats to the walk of shame. Jesus, you got a real Cagney streak in ya, don't ya, kid? I take back what I said, this plan puts mine to shame."

"Yeah, now let's just hope it actually works. It's pretty ambitious, and you know how things can go wrong."

"You're some kinda genius, kid."

"Thanks, Harry, but let's see if it works first. Let the show begin."

* * *

Watching the muted chaos inside the station, Lorene has a memory of walking through that door one day, one of the last days she was on duty before the boys got back from Europe. The way it was so quiet in the morning before anyone else got there, the darkened streets humming; the only other person she'd encounter was the red-eyed night cop, usually a woman named Peggy Sue Johnson, a hotel desk clerk who was used to working nights anyway and so didn't mind much passing the dark hours doing nothing but reading trashy paperbacks. The two of them would exchange nods, never saying much, the unspoken bond between them forged by misogyny and wartime progress-as-necessity.

Inside the police station, the first signs of distress begin to run across a couple of the cops' faces. Even through the glare of the window, Lorene and Harry can both see the look play across their features: their mouths tightening, eyes bulging just a little, backs straightening, movements brought to bare minimum, weaving around the chaos and the snaking line of Jehovahs scattered around the station. The missionaries all begin to withdraw slowly, one at a time, either finishing their spiels or simply dropping them. From their vantage point, Lorene can't tell if the look on the cops' faces is confusion or discomfort. More pinched expressions, more urgent fidgeting. More cops begin toward the bathroom area. Lines begin to form; the first ones to make it in begin to make their way out, looking drained and sickly. Harry and Lorene can see them talking to the ones waiting in line, the ones who are gripping their stomachs or shuffling in place or squatting and squeezing their backsides tightly.

"Oh God, kid, you think they tellin em the toilets ain't workin? I wonder what yer plumber pal did."

A couple of the officers, Krieger among them, push past and into the restrooms, broken toilets be damned apparently. Smith waddles out from his office to join the growing chaos in the narrow hallway.

"I thought Smith had his own private shitter?"

"He does," Lorene says, and holds up a polished silver door handle. "But it's virtually impossible to open without this."

"Holy hell, kid, I didn't even see you take it! That's some slick shit... You should go into the magic business or somethin."

Cops have begun leaning on desks, faces in agony. Smith is yelling something. He pushes his way into one of the bathrooms. Nothing changes for a few long moments.

"Damn...maybe them toilets ain't actually outta comission."

A rumble below Lorene and Harry instantly silences them both.

"The hell was that? Some part a yer plan ya fergot ta tell me about? Some kinda elephant or somethin? You got a Cthulhu you waitin to bring out? I think yer takin this prank a little too far, kid—"

"I don't have anything else up my sleeve, Harry. That isn't me."

They feel the rumble again, this time stronger, followed by another in quick succession.

"Kid…" Harry points toward the station. An officer bursts through the front door, waddling into the street in a half-crouch, holding his ass in his hands.

"Oh, well, I guess this is our first—" Lorene begins, but stops as the officer begins screaming. His inaudible barking becomes words as he squats across the center line.

"I'm shitting in the street! I'M SHITTING IN THE STREET!"

"Holy, uh…well, *shit*, kid…"

With a roar and the sound of gravy sucked up through a straw, the manhole cover between the station and Harry's car explodes, sending a brown geyser spraying into the air.

"Uh," Harry utters. Another loud sound, an explosion from inside the station, and officers pour out en masse, followed by a wave of brownish liquid, gallons of it, *a river of it*, Harry would remark later. Screams from every direction, the first officer who had made it out swept off his feet by the chunky splashing. He tries to stand but simply kneels in the knee-high pool that forms around him.

The officers left inside are drenched and dripping, running around the station. Some have ripped their pants off and are hovering over trash cans, open desk drawers; one has emptied a flower vase and is trying, mostly unsuccessfully, to direct his output into the small opening. Some of the officers are simply rolling in the receding muck, screaming, crying, holding their stomachs and asses. They see Chief Smith pull himself from the burbling brown pool as it slowly dissipates into the storm gutters, into yards, splattering across lawn gnomes and staining white picket fences with a thick mud. He wipes a clump of something from his face, a small wad of toilet paper still stuck to his upper lip. He looks directly at Harry and Lorene.

More screams erupt, small and high-pitched, honking in a chorus of unintelligible noises. Lorene finds the source: a group of children gathered behind the windows of the elementary school across the street from the police station, their faces pressed against the glass in horror and disgust at the scene before them. The brown spew. The flow and ebb and cries. The gurgling. Some children cover their eyes; some can't tear them away from the hideousness playing out in the street. Lorene sees one keel over as if vomiting, and it echoes around the other faces Lorene can see through the window, some gushing across the dirty glass, some heaving over and out of sight, one begets two, then four, then ten. A rush of liquids to match those outside their small school building.

"Holy shit, kid, we gotta get the fuck outta here! Now!"

"Good call, Harry. This got a little out of hand."

"You can say that again."

As Harry peels off, avoiding the brown river washing its way out of the street, Lorene sees the *Happy Birthday* banner float out the station door, followed by the picture that had hung in the lobby. Behind it, the fading moans and sobs of the town's police force, bubbling with mouthfuls of the brown muck slowly dribbling away.

7

LORENE KEEPS RECOUNTING everything in her mind as she and Harry sit silently in the office, Harry shuffling through paperwork distractedly.

"Heh-heh... *I'm shittin in the street.* Lord help me," Harry mutters almost under his breath, chuckling and looking up at Lorene. "Remind me never ta double-cross you."

The phone's pulsating ring almost makes Lorene jump. Harry answers it gruffly. "Ypsilanti's office. Yeah. Okay. Aw, shit. Okay, no, I got it. I'll be there right away. Thanks for callin... Bye." Harry sighs heavily as he hangs up the phone. "So... One more fer tha day. But there's a catch. This one's kinda, well, personal. It's my little brother. He's...well, he's got some issues. I gotta go give him a hand fore someone calls the cops on him, although, after what you did to em, they might all be down for a day or two at least. Look, kid, I understand if you wanna head home, I'm passing by yer side a town, so I can drop ya off if ya want."

"I'll come with you, if you want me to. It's not like I have anything better to do on an afternoon like this."

"Great, kid. Let me grab my coat and take a quick puffer or two, keep me level-headed."

* * *

Harry's little brother, Ralphie, looks almost exactly like him. Tall, pot-bellied, jowled. Ralphie lacks the rough five o'clock shadow Harry always wears, and his eyes aren't Harry's hard and darting slits, but even so, from a distance you can hardly tell the two apart, aside from Ralphie's apparent penchant for shouting and the track marks running up and down his arms. When Lorene and Harry arrive, Ralphie is attempting to light his garage on fire with a box of matches.

"Hey, Ralphie, how ya doin? Just wanted ya ta meet my new partner, Lorene."

Lorene waves as casually as she can to Ralphie, who has turned to stare at the two of them, swaying.

"Wash you stay to meesh?!" Ralphie mumbles. Lorene doesn't understand what he says, but Harry seems to be used to this strange, slurred dialect.

"I said meet Lorene. She's my new partner. C'mon, buddy, let's go inside for a bit, you can tell me—"

"No! No inside!"

"Okay, buddy, no inside. We'll stay right here."

"No inside. The villains…are out here. Must remain vigilant," Ralphie says, momentarily lucid and understandable.

"Okay, okay, let's just keep it calm, Ralphie, fore somebody calls the fuzz on us. Let's go do a viper, relax, you know how smokin always calms you down, right? Let's do that and—"

"Hahahaahahah! You fugin theenk yute can bride me? Whiff dat, druds… Smokin drugs… You can't. Can't tempt the consemution of the Justice Judicator!"

"Ralphie, buddy, you gotta listen ta yer older brother, now. Ya just drank too much, yer havin another one'a yer episodes. Ya gotta listen ta what I'm sayin to ya!"

Ralphie puts a broken cigarette in his mouth, filter end out. He raises the matches, struggling to get one lit. He stops and looks up at Harry, his eyes suddenly clear, focusing.

"I'm cold, Harry… Are you cold?" Ralphie asks quietly.

"No, buddy, I'm actually a little warm. Here, take my coat." Harry drapes his coat around his brother gently, and despite everything she knows about him, Lorene thinks in that moment he looks almost parental again.

"I'm gonna run inside and grab him a glass of water, can you make sure he don't go nowhere?"

"Sure thing, Harry."

"The streets…are quiet tonight. Almost too quiet," Ralphie says in a deep, gravelly voice. He whips the trenchcoat around like a cape.

"So, you…you keep these streets safe?" Lorene asks, unsure how to engage the man.

"Indeed, young lady, protector of justice and the night here in Forest Rapids, I am the Justice Judicator!" As Ralphie says this, holes begin appearing in Harry's trenchcoat, and Ralphie twists and shakes, looking to Lorene for a split-second as if he is dancing until the sound of gunshots catches up to the optics. Lorene leaps behind Harry's car, bullets raining next to and above her, somehow not hitting her. Tires screech, the firing stops, and Lorene is up and shooting, striking the rear of the car speeding past, the vehicle continuing without even slowing.

Harry runs from inside the house with his gun drawn. "The fuck happened? Ralphie!"

Harry rushes to his fallen brother. Crimson speckles among the reptilian-green of the grass, Ralphie a dark motionless shape half-covered in tattered trenchcoat.

"Somebody just drove up and started shooting, then took off! I hit the car a couple times, but…" Lorene trails off, voice full of the stuff just before crying, her breathing that quickened shuddering just on the edge of sobs.

"Ralphie! Ralphie, hang in there, buddy!"

* * *

Lorene had already wondered if Harry would ever let her drive his car. She never could have imagined it would be like this, terror pulsing through her veins, Ralphie's blood covering her hands clamped to the steering wheel, his screams from the backseat mingling with Harry's soothing babble, white lies to try to calm his brother down. Things he had no way of knowing if they were true.

Peeling around corners dangerously, tires screaming twangy squeals, pressing the gas pedal as far down as she dared for as long as she could pretend it was slightly "safe" to, hoping no one happened into the street in front of her, or no cops were lurking about to find her leaving the speed limit behind as a lost thought.

"C'mon, kid, we gotta go!"

"Yeah, Harry, I'm going as fast as I can! We're almost there! Just another couple streets!"

* * *

"How tha fuck do ya mean tha hospital's closed?! How in the hell you just *close* a hospital?!"

"Sir, you need to calm down now. I'm sorry, but as I said, the hospital is not closed, just under temporary quarantine. A number of people were brought in with a severe stomach ailment. Most of the town's police officers, actually, and protocol dictates we have to seal the place up until we ID what's going on," says the staff person outside the caution tape and plastic sheets covering the building's entrance.

"So what the hell do we do wit him?! He's fulla fuckin bullets and leakin his innards out all over my fuckin backseat!" Harry looks back at the car, his brother propped up in the backseat, motionless.

"I'm sorry, sir, there's nothing I can do. No one goes in or out till I get the all-clear. You'll just have to take him to Wayward Pines County Hospital."

"Wayward Pines is almost twenty miles away! He'll never make it! He's my brother!" Harry bellows, standing taller and puffing himself out like a bear or a cat about to pounce.

"I can help him." A voice, a short distance away. Harry and Lorene search for the source. A short, stocky woman steps from around the corner, dressed in a flowing gown and wearing a number of strange beads and trinkets around her neck.

"Who the hell are you?" Lorene asks.

"I am just a lonely soul longing to heal. A discarded relic, if you will, who uses other discarded relics to mend, to make better. Make whole. Traveling the soft back of the wind," the woman says as she gets closer to Lorene and Harry. Lorene catches a mixture of rotten fruit and nag champa radiating from the woman.

"I dunno what any of that means. Are you a doctor?" Harry asks.

"In some people's eyes."

"The fuck does that mean? You a doctor or not?" Harry asks impatiently.

"We are all doctors without the placards, if we know the right medicine." The woman waves her hand as if in a meaningful way. Harry turns to Lorene and only lowers his voice slightly.

"You get a fucked-up vibe from this one?"

"I dunno… I think she's mad. We probably shouldn't let her anywhere near Ralphie," Lorene says.

"Yeah, but how many other options we got?" Harry looks between the old woman and Ralphie in the backseat, who is picking his nose and looking at the reddish-green clump that comes out.

"Quickly, your brother is dying. Bring him this way if you want to save him!"

"Fine. We'll be right behind you," Harry barks.

***

In back of the hospital, near where they keep the dumpsters, Harry pulls the car up next to the battered RV the old woman stands behind. The brown paint on the sides is chipped and cracked with age. The spare tire cover on the rear reads *Magadelene Cromickey, Write-In Candidate for President* in fading blue and red lettering.

"Take him inside, and I will get some supplies. Put him on the table in the kitchen."

Harry and Lorene hoist Ralphie, now drifting in and out of consciousness, onto the table. Through the small camper window, Harry sees the old woman dive headlong into one of the large dumpsters.

"Holy shit, kid, this dingus mighta just went off tha deep end! You stay here, I'll be right back!" Harry races toward the dumpsters, and Lorene watches through the small camper window. A large brown banana flies from the dumpster and lands on the ground in front of Harry, splattering the pavement in a greyish-black goo.

"What the hell're ya doin?" Harry yells up at the lip of the dumpster. Something else flies out from it, an indeterminate glob of muck, almost striking Harry in the face. Trash rains down on him, and he leaps nimbly between the gooey projectiles. "Ya crazy old bird, what in the hell do ya—"

"Begin collecting the supplies. We'll need them to save your brother."

"Supplies? Lady, this is garbage. From tha dumpster. Maybe you havin one a them dissociative fugue states, I get those sometimes. Come on down outta there." Harry stares up at the dumpster for a few moments in disbelief. More trash falls like snowflakes, and Harry realizes he won't get any other answer. He begins scooping the most intact chunks of garbage from the warm concrete. Flies have descended on the scene already, and Harry swats at them as he tries to load his arms with rotting baubles.

Lorene watches as Harry brings armful after armful of whatever the hell the old woman was chucking out of the dumpster. He begins to amass a sick wet pile just inside the RV's door, the smell trapping in the tiny enclosed box, beginning to permeate Lorene's nostrils like a fire, mixing with the smell of old cigarettes and blood that already made a pungent cocktail on the sweltering air.

"Harry, what the hell are you doing? What is all this?" Lorene asks as Harry steps inside and drops off another armload with a gut-rolling slurping sound.

"I have no fuckin clue, kid," Harry says without stopping.

* * *

After what feels like hours of the old woman tossing filth down to Harry, she finally has enough of whatever it is she is looking for. The woman enters the RV covered in a thick black slime, like mucus run through coffee grounds, leaving a thin trail behind her as she steps through the vehicle into the bedroom.

"Grab some of the pile, a good armload, and bring it to the table. Girl, get Ralphie's shirt off and run a glass of warm but not hot water," the old woman calls from the back of the RV. Lorene hears the sound of hands digging through some kind of trunk or dresser. The old woman returns with something clutched in the palm of her hand. "Now, you rub the mixture into his wounds, while you, girl, dribble water onto his face. Little bits at a time."

"The hell will that do?" Harry asks.

"And, excuse me for asking, as I'm not a doctor or anything, but should you be putting rotting garbage on his open wounds? And what about the bullets—?" Lorene begins.

"Now is not the time for questions; do you want to save this man's life or not?! Do as I tell you. Both of you!" the old woman interrupts.

Harry begins rubbing the putrid slop in his hands into the small leaking holes in his brother's exposed chest. Ralphie screams, not opening his eyes, and Lorene begins pouring small amounts of water onto his face. The old woman opens her palm to reveal three small crystals, differing in size and shape. She puts one in Ralphie's hand and closes his fingers around it.

"Here, this is for you. Don't let go of it." The woman takes another crystal and reaches around behind her. The noise of a half-melted push-pop pressed out of its sleeve, and then the old woman titters quietly. "And this one goes here…"

"The hell did you just stick that crystal, lady?" Harry asks.

"Now, this last one needs to be waved over his body while you two work," the woman says, ignoring Harry.

Lorene scowls at this. "Crystals?"

"Keep going, girl. You have no idea the power crystals hold."

"I mean, I get the idea behind it, I've done some crystal healing in my day. But for gunshot wounds? Are they *that* strong?" Harry asks, not taking his eyes from his brother's face as he works more of the gelatinous black semi-liquid into Ralphie's wounds. Harry sees a small chunk of what is likely putrid bacon fall from one of the holes he has just rubbed with gunk.

"They are indeed. The crystals—" the old woman begins as the door to the RV flies open. A tall, thin figure steps inside.

"Is everything okay? I heard screami— OH MY GOD! What the hell are you people doing in here?! What are you doing to this man?!"

"Everything is fine, we've got it under control!" the old woman says hastily.

"This man is my brother, he's been shot. The hospital is under quarantine, so this, uh, this kind woman offered ta…help…"

"Help? Help put him out of his misery? What in the fuck are you even doing? Are you rubbing garbage into his wounds?! Was that her idea?" the new woman asks, slapping the older woman's hand away from Ralphie's shaking form.

"It is a medicine I learned from my mother's people," the old woman says, matter-of-factly.

"Your mother's people? Who, the goddamn mole people?! You work at PJ's Groceries, you've lived here your whole life! Grab that man and bring him over to my clinic right now, if you want any hope of saving him."

"The treatment works... I've seen it work."

"This man needs medical attention now! He will die if we don't operate immediately! C'mon!" The younger woman leads Lorene and Harry, who are carrying Ralphie between themselves, across the street and over to her small clinic. "I mostly am an OBGYN, but I guarantee I've got way more experience with life-threatening injuries than that psychopath does."

"Whatever you can do, Doc, please. I can't lose my little brother...he's all I got left."

8

LORENE WATCHES HARRY as he sits quietly over Ralphie's sleeping form. The doctor's office is trashed, covered in blood and bandages, used instruments, mud and puddles of trash and various other gunk they had pulled from Ralphie's four bullet wounds. His chest rises and falls in a slow rhythm.

"It sounds like they'll be re-opening the hospital soon; I told them to send an ambulance over as soon as they do, we can get Ralphie transferred over there. But it looks like he's going to make it. Probably a few cases of septicemia from the garbage, he'll probably want to get tested for hep C, syphilis, Rocky Mountain spotted fever, maybe bubonic plague, just to be safe, but other than that..."

"Thanks, Doc. That old quack and her garbage, I can't believe we listened to her..."

"When someone we love is in danger, we don't always think straight. Don't sweat it. I'm just glad I found you all before she did any more damage." She puts a sympathetic hand on Harry's shoulder.

Harry smiles at the doctor. Ralphie coughs and blinks his eyes open.

"Harry...?"

"Ralphie, buddy, I'm right here. How you doin?"

"I'm...okay, Harry. Did she fix me? Was it the magic of fermentation that saved my life?"

"Well, uh, no, buddy, the doc here patched you up. Turns out Lady Garbage didn't give ya much more'n a case a crabs. No, real medicine fixed ya up this time, buddy. You're gonna make it."

"Of course I'll make it. I was able to use my superior super-human abilities and skills to position my body perfectly so the penetrating bullets hit no vital organs. You would not have fared so well."

"Me? What the hell does that mean?"

"I was wearing your costume, Harry. Surely the evildoers mistook me for you."

Harry looks thoughtfully at his brother for a moment. "Huh, my coat... Who the hell'd wanna kill me, doh?"

* * *

"You gonna be okay, Harry?" Lorene asks. They're standing outside Doctor Gooding's clinic as the ambulance drivers load Ralphie into the back.

"Oh yeah. You go home and get some rest, kid. I got some heavy thinkin ta do."

"Is that, like, a euphemism for something?"

"Oh, yeah, it means I'ma go back ta my place and smoke reefers till I pass out. Get some rest, kid, and tomorrow we're gonna figure out who tha fuck shot my little brother," Harry says, lighting another cigarette.

"Are you sure that's such a good idea? I mean, we only have like two cases it could be, maybe we should just stop poking around *both* of them, call them both unsolved, move on..."

"Move on ta what, goin back ta pullin cats outta trees and gettin lost in some weirdo's fuckin museum a old TV dinners and mummified pets? Nah, I think we found somethin real here. A case *worth* solvin, if we can figure out which one they tryna scare us offa. And we gotta be getting close, kid, for whoever did it to risk a public hit like that..."

"Okay, Harry... I'm in. I need to see where this goes. What else am I gonna do around here anyway? Besides, we've seen how great Forest Rapids' finest are at their jobs, and if this really is some kind of...conspiracy? Nefarious plot? Whatever it is, they won't be able to handle it. And you can't. Not alone."

"You're right, kid, I'm lost without a partner. So whaddya say we start bright and early tomorrow...for real bright and early. Nine o'clock, maybe?"

"Harry Ypsilanti, I am shocked to even hear those words leave your lips. I'm going to hold you to it."

"Shit, maybe I shoulda said ten."

"Ah, too late. See you at nine."

"Okay, nine it is. Be careful, kid."

"You too, Harry."

* * *

Restless, Lorene finally gets up from her fitful non-sleep and finds the empty sidewalk an open canvas for tossing her thoughts at, trying combinations and new paths, thinking through the events of the last few days, keeping the corners of her eyes alert for passing cars, signs of anything amiss. She turns a corner and stops to peer in a shop window, a small ventriloquist's doll smiling back at her, her reflection hovering just above its shining, transfixed stare.

"Well, that's terrifying."

The sound of footsteps continues behind her. Not her own. Getting closer. Lorene continues, trying to keep her pace casual, but all focus diverted like dammed streams to listening for the sound of someone else's shoes. Rounding the corner. Matching her speed, intentionally falling back, staying hidden. Or maybe just heading in a similar direction, maybe seeing someone ahead of you simply sets a pace. It doesn't feel like it. And with what happened to Ralphie earlier, Lorene isn't taking any chances.

Lorene ducks down an alleyway, picks her way through a maze of garbage cans and crates. She stops and turns after she gets about halfway down, and sees a man round the corner. He stops in the darkness. In the shadows, his face is every ghost story Lorene had ever read, every monster she'd seen on the silver screen. Every bump in the night of her youth and her adulthood.

"Who the hell are you? Why are you following me?" Lorene yells down the alley, her legs tensing, ready to begin carrying her as soon as anything triggered them to. No answer; the figure just steps forward toward her, slowly, as if darkness itself moving. *Fuck this.* Legs running before both words race across her mind, in her voice, the fear audible like a halo around them inside her brain. Down the alley, around another corner, some small animal leaping and darting away from her in terror. Behind her the footsteps quicken, but the man isn't running...yet.

Around another bend, hopefully heading back out toward Superior Street, busy enough to have someone driving or walking. Lorene debates shouting for help when she sees someone ahead of her. A cop. Leaning against the wall, smoking, not noticing the woman barreling toward him.

"Officer, please! That man back there, he's following me, and I think—"

"That man? Let's see what's going on here," the officer says. Lorene doesn't recognize the cop, but he looks larger than the person chasing her. Not all of Smith's boys are bumbling. The officer tosses his cigarette to the ground heroically and stands from the wall.

"Oh...shit," Lorene gasps out loud. The officer is only wearing the front of a police uniform. His exposed ass drops little chunks of dirt as it lifts from the brick it is pressed against, a pocked pattern engraved in it from the wall's texture. The officer smiles at her and begins toward the figure, who has stopped a few meters away, partially lit by a dim streetlamp between them.

"Lollipops and garter belts, mister! Whistles of the wind! This young lady tells me you been spitoonin' your creamed corn… That's gestapo's gazpacho, that is!" the officer says as he approaches the other man.

"Wait!" Lorene calls after him. The figure pushes the ersatz officer over into a pile of trash bags, and Lorene begins running before she can see what he will do next. She yells up at the darkened windows, to no answer. Ahead of her, a dead end looms. On just the other side must be Superior Street. *Damn it.* Lorene stops near the end, looking for some way out. Fire escapes all pulled up out of reach. Most doors look too solid to kick in. Why the hell'd she leave her gun back at the office? Stupid mistake. Harry'd be disappointed. *He will be, kid, when he finds yer corpse all mangled and blood-sucked tomorrow when he actually gets up bright and early…* Her inner voice mocks Harry's ridiculous, unplaceable accent, but out of what is fast becoming some kind of friendship. She is actually growing to like the idiot a little, or at least be able to tolerate him.

Maybe she could bust out a bottom window in one of these buildings, if she could find one she could actually fit through. *I could start throwing rocks at windows like a teenage boy…*

A light flicks on behind one of the doors.

"Hello, is someone there?" Lorene calls. Behind her the figure closes the distance between them with slow, long strides. As he gets closer, Lorene sees the strangeness of his features. The way his skin seems too smooth. The way the eyes look, like they are soggy and stretched. The twisted, wet, red-gummed smile.

"Fine. Nowhere else to run. I'm not gonna make this easy for you, motherfucker. You might take me. But you might not." Lorene squares off at the smiling man, and tries to mimic the crazed look in his eyes, the warp of his lips; tries to out-psychopath him.

"Um…is everything okay out here?" A woman stands in the now-open doorway behind Lorene. She crosses her arms and looks at the two people standing in the alley.

"No, actually it's not," Lorene says, and backs slowly toward the open door, not taking her eyes off the approaching figure. "I don't know who this creep is, but he's been following me since Georgia Street."

"Okay, pal, you had your fun, you scared the little lady. Now get the fuck outta here. Go find some other way of getting your sick rocks off…preferably alone, as far from any other women as you can, you fucking perv. This is your only warning," the woman says.

"Thanks," Lorene says.

The man's smile never wavers, and he continues his approach. He looks between Lorene and the woman, and begins laughing. A grating, twisted sound. Twirled around old bones and swamp vines. Padded with rocks and rotten fruit. Chunks of broken glass stuck in a chorus of throats. Laughing that almost isn't laughing. That is almost growling. Almost screaming. Almost the sound a body makes splattering concrete from twenty stories up. He takes another step forward, slowing a little as he stares directly into Lorene's eyes.

A chunk of his shoulder explodes outward, followed immediately by the thick crack of a gunshot. The man grunts and falls backward, blood hanging in the air in a misty smoke cloud for a brief moment above him.

"Holy shit!" Lorene calls, covering her ears too late, shaking her head at the gentle ringing as the noise dies down.

"I warned him. Can't be too careful with creeps like that, especially in this day and age. I heard Nazis are coming back. Nazis, can you believe it? I thought we got rid a them with the end of the war. Apparently they're Americans now, just like you and me, except somehow, something in em turns…bad. Can you believe that?" The woman smirks.

"Huh. That's, uh, that's not good."

"Yeah. You don't think he's a Nazi, do ya?"

"No, I don't think so. I mean, maybe, but I don't think that's why he's chasing me."

"Well, the name's Carolina. Would you maybe like a cup of coffee or anything?"

"Honestly, I could use something stronger after this, if that isn't too forward of me…?"

"You got it—" Carolina is cut off as the man leaps up, grunting like a cornered animal. She raises the hand cannon and fires another shot, just missing the man's leg as he turns and flees back down the alley. Carolina chases after him around the corner. A moment later she returns, the weapon held casually at her side. She stops where the man had fallen, squatting and examining the dark green puddle on the concrete. She frowns. "Huh?"

"*Huh* what?" Lorene asks, the ringing in her ears beginning to fade into static prickling all around her.

"Somethin weird about this guy's blood. Let's have a drink and we'll look a little closer."

"Okay," Lorene says skeptically.

"So, I got bourbon, scotch, and gin. What's your fancy?"

* * *

It takes Harry a long time to answer the telephone as Lorene and Carolina sit in a modestly decorated dining room, a framed Egon Schiele painting hung neatly on the wall, the only color and sense of disorder among the clean and minimal aesthetic. They both sip Tom Collinses, and Lorene smokes a cigarette as she holds the telephone to her ear.

When he finally does pick up, after too many rings for Lorene to count, Harry sounds groggy and terse.

"Huh? What da hell is it? This better not be that Franks kid again, ya hear me?! I ain't gonna buy none a yer goddamn *Family Newspapers*, ya little shit!"

"What—uh, Harry, it's me."

"Oh, Jesus—kid? I mean, kid-kid? What brings ya ta ringin my house at two in da mornin? Everything okay?"

After Lorene tells Harry what happened, he suddenly sounds very sober and very alert. It doesn't take him long to arrive at Carolina's doorstep.

"You okay?" Harry asks as he steps inside.

"Yeah, thanks to Carolina. She winged the guy, scared him off…"

"Winged him, like hell. I hit him dead to rights; his ass jumped up and took off running, like I just hit him with a BB gun."

Harry looks the woman over and smiles. "Well, thanks. I just got this new partner, and I'd hate ta hafta find another one so soon."

"She's almost killed by some doped-up goon and that's all you have to say? *I don wanna finda new partna*," Carolina mimics.

"Hey look, lady, I'm here, ain't I? This is me tryin. Ain't like I got a lotta practice with this kinda stuff. I'm glad you're okay, kid, I really am." Harry glares at Carolina. "And not just as a partner. I'm glad you're okay, y'know, as a friend too." Harry looks as if he is blushing as he says this. Carolina smirks. "There, ya happy now?"

"Thanks, Harry. I just feel like an idiot for leaving my gun."

"Don't sweat it, kid, you ain't a superhero, you can't be on point all the time. Now, let's go take a look at the spot you dropped this creep. You said somethin about green blood?"

9

LORENE HASN'T BEEN up this early since her days on the force. Blueish purple smoke hovering the sky, horizon a salmon light spreading like oil plume, like a pastel crowd pushing onto the street from a subway stop.

"Let's grab a couple coffees and somethin fer breakfast. Not sure my brain is a hundred percent fired up yet, I dunno about you. Who in the name a Jesus'd wanna get up this early…ever?"

"Yeah, Harry, that sounds good, I could use some coffee. I didn't get much sleep last night, after everything. So what the hell do we do now?"

"We keep goin with the runaway case, is what we do now."

"After everything that's happened? You really think that's a good idea?"

"Yeah, they tryna scare us…that means we're close. I can feel it. The only problem is, I'm almost outta leads. Apparently her gran sometimes takes her in when she's 'run off' before, though she claims Trisha isn't there. Hopefully this old lady knows somethin… anythin. Otherwise, we're about outta options."

***

One house looks just like the rest, small and pastel-colored, boxed in by each other and the little fenced-in yards. When Harry knocks on the door, it pushes open slowly.

"Shit scabs… Here we go, I guess," Harry says quietly, drawing his pistol, and Lorene follows suit. "Hello? Anyone home?"

The inside of the house is clean and sparsely decorated: white furniture, light grey carpets look like they've never been walked on, the walls spackled with a bright yellow floral pattern, light pushing in from the bay window. Everything is still and quiet as they step inside.

"Hello? I don't think anyone's here. Let's split up. You take the two bedrooms, I'll take the kitchen, laundry room, bathroom. God, please don't let this one be dead too."

"Okay, I guess."

"That not agree with you, kid?"

"It's just, why are we splitting up? This house is so small…"

"To cover more ground! If you want the kitchen and—"

"It's fine, Harry."

Lorene begins to make her way toward the back bedrooms. Harry looks around the kitchen, picking up a pastrami sandwich and raising it to his face as if to take a bite.

"Uh, Harry?" Lorene calls from across the small house.

"What's up, kid? You find Granny? She dead? Put a blanket over her if she's dead, kid, I can't take that right now, it's too goddamn early." Harry throws the sandwich back down onto the counter.

"Harry?"

"What? Jesus, I'm comin, give me a seco—" Harry turns the corner out of the kitchen and is cut off by a wet, slick flash. Something long and thick and slimy slaps him in the face, leaving a trail of goo slathered across it. Like seaweed and bloody stool. Mucus but sand-filled. Little teeth. Harry raises his pistol and ducks into a crouch below the reaching, worm-like thing.

"You okay, kid? Where you at? There's some kinda, ah, thing, out here."

"Yeah, Harry, I'm fine. I'm in the bathroom. There's something in here too," Lorene calls. Harry steps slowly around the tentacle and finds Lorene inside the bathroom, standing in front of an old woman sitting calmly on the toilet, a number of tentacles pulsating out from beneath her.

"Jesus Christ! What is it?" Harry asks, pointing his weapon at the woman on the toilet, who doesn't seem to notice him. Lorene opens her mouth to answer, and is swept out the bathroom window by the one of the tentacles in a quick flicking movement. "Whoa-ly shit! Lorene, kid, you all right?"

"Yeah… I'm fine. I'll be back in in a second," Lorene calls from the side yard.

"Lady, what the fuck is goin on here?!"

"Oh, my… I think my hemorrhoids must be actin up again," the old woman says quietly.

"Lady, I don't think it was hemorrhoids just flung my partner through the window!"

"What's that? I left my hearing aids in the bedroom."

"I said—" Harry begins to bellow, and one of the tentacles stops flailing and begins to look as if it is melting in front of his face. The melt becomes ridges and indentations, becomes flaps and folds, lumps and lashes. Lips and the slick pointed teeth beneath. Eyes not human, glassy and cold. Full of moonlight and the sheen on top of tar pits. A face, but not one. Something worse. A face, but a scream as well. The smell of garbage simmering in summer sun, of old cooking oil caking around cracked sidewalk eggs. Harry looks up at it, eye-level with the face or whatever it is.

"Oh, shit."

The face cracks a smile at Harry's words. "Oh…shit…"

Before it can say anything else, Harry fires three times in rapid succession, striking the tentacle with all three bullets, tearing jagged holes through it, sending greenish spatter across the wall, the pink fuzzy toilet seat cover, the old woman's white slippers, her exposed buttocks, all across Harry's front-side. The other tentacles begin whipping wildly, and one begins to melt, another face forming beneath the dripping and thrashing.

"Young man, could you please pass me the Preparation H?" the old woman asks, still seemingly oblivious to the chaos around her. The tentacle with the face turns to look at her.

"Pre…par…a…tion… H," it gasps and hisses, horrible mimic of human speech.

"Yes, it should be in the medicine cabinet. Thank you very much, young man," the woman responds to the tentacled face that has just attempted speaking.

Harry leaps backward through the doorway, narrowly avoiding the whip-thrash of another tentacle.

"Uh, we'll be right back, lady, just, you know, stay calm… Uh, don't push it, uh…and wipe front to back, I guess."

Lorene reaches Harry in the hallway.

"C'mon, kid, we gotta get the hell gone, there's some freaky shit happenin in that bathroom. This lady needs an exterminator…or an exorcist, maybe."

"So we're just gonna leave her in there like that?"

"What the hell else we gonna do? You know how to stop those things? It ain't gonna do none a us any good we go back in there and one a them wormy-arm things decides to snap our little necks. We'll call the cops, let them know—as if they'll believe a word a this—and we'll go find someone who might know what this thing is."

"Who might know what this thing is?" Lorene asks as one of the tentacles smashes through the wall and wavers at them as it melts and forms a face, just as the other two did. "Uh… What the fuck?"

"Wh…at the…fu…uck," it globbers.

"Yeah, they do that. I might know someone, a…friend, I guess you could say. Someone I've had, uh, dealings with. He's not the most respectable guy on the block, but nothin majorly offensive, some drugs here and there, some gamblin stuff, the usual soft-racket stuff. Dealin stolen merchandise…"

"Sounds like a real winner, Harry."

"Hey, I don't condone it, that's fer sure. But he don't hurt people or nothin, plus he's a good source. And I told him, *I* ever catch him doin anything, I'm gonna have ta take him in. He just laughs when I say that, but he knows I mean that shit. A little rule bending, a little tomfoolery, a little fast and loose with the law is fine by me, but there is a line I don't cross. You get on the other side a it…ain't no way we can be buddies no more."

"Okay…so who is this sort-of friend who's sort of a criminal?"

"His name is Dudeford Trevor McMicheals… the Third."

"Is he a comic book villain?"

"No, he's…a southern gentleman."

* * *

The house is an old, decrepit-looking manor on the edge of town Lorene had never noticed before, sitting far back from a tall, thick hedge that might be hiding a wall beneath. Vines creep across the front of the house, snaking along the top of the lopsided wooden porch. A small gate seems to be the only way through the hedge.

"So how do we get in?" Lorene asks, looking around for some other sign of driveway.

"We walk, kid."

"All the way up to the house? That's gotta be almost a mile."

"Nah, it's three quarters of a mile, tops. Easy as pie, kid. C'mon. If an old man like me can do it, should be no sweat for you."

Lorene resents this exaggeration as they reach the front porch and the man sitting on it, motionless, watching the pair make their way up the driveway. Lorene's breath is broken stutters, struggling to fill the bags in her chest. The back of her throat tastes like citrus, the flesh of her esophagus raw and throbbing gently. Sweat stains her shirt, drips from her forehead down into her eyes, stinging and somehow cooling at the same time.

"Young Master Ypsilanti…and some type of squire, perhaps?" The man on the porch untangles his long thin limbs and stands from the chair as he says this. He is tall, wearing a perfectly neat purple suit, the sparkle of jewelry across his fingers, encircling his wrists. He is cleanly shaven and wears a shiny black top hat, looming near the porch's sagging wooden ceiling.

"Uh, yeah, Dudee, this is, uh, Lorene Brandt. I'm, uh, training her."

"A pleasure to make your acquaintance. Please, both of you, come in. Mint juleps?"

* * *

Mint juleps all around as they sit at an ornate redwood table, polished to a glassy surface, reflecting Lorene's face back up at her. Music dribbles softly from somewhere, Lorene can't quite place it. A young red-haired boy stands looking bored behind Dudeford, waving a large fan at him. Lorene shifts uncomfortably as she watches the boy. *What the hell is this?*

"So, Dudee, as always, great ta see ya. I'm a jump right ta business taday, if that's all right, we're kinda in a hurry…"

"Certainly. Are you sure I can't interest either of you in a fan child? They are quite wonderful."

"Uh, as temptin as that is," Harry begins.

"Look, Mr. McMicheals, sir, I know we've only just met, but I can't sit here while children—"

"Oh, Ms. Brandt, I will stop you right there. I think you are misunderstanding the nature of these boys' service to me. There is nothing *untoward* going on here. I pay my fan children a very fair living wage, and they work within all youth labor guidelines. Are you happy here, boy?" Dudeford turns and looks to the child behind him, who smiles and nods.

"Yeah, it's pretty swell."

"And the children's parent or guardian is just in the other room, watching television. So you see, there is nothing to feel unethical or immoral about here. My fan children are completely in compliance with the law."

"But why kids? Why not have adults do it? Or, I don't know…mechanical fans? Like the rest of us," Lorene asks, barely hiding the contention in her voice.

"Ah, because, Ms. Brandt, there is a special magic in the arms of children. It is like a good wine; certainly; almost any wine will get you drunk, if that is all you wish for. A great many might even taste halfway decent. But when you find that special combination of grape, and soil, and process…there is something distinct and magical in that taste. That is why I use children."

Lorene doesn't know how to respond to this, and Harry steps in to turn the conversation before it gets further off course.

"So, Dudee, hate ta keep harpin on ya, but back ta that business— some weird shit's goin on around town. And today, we seen tha A1 Duke a Weird Shit comin outta some old lady's asshole. I was hopin you might a heard somethin around town, talk of like…weird tentacle monsters, or somethin. Maybe, like, ones that talk and shit?"

"You mean like Kassogtha? Perhaps it was an ancient entity you encountered."

"I mean, I dunno about ancient entities, but they was definitely tentacles from somethin. It was more like, this lady was transformin *into* somethin. And dey grew faces and everything."

"Interesting. I have not heard anything on the proverbial grapevine."

"What about the motherfucker who shot my brother? We think this might all be related to that, and this case we been workin on, the runaway I told you about… It's all tied together, I know it is."

"I did find an interesting tidbit about that, my gumshoe friend. The brutes who pulled the trigger… They're a part of the Silly Putty gang. They like to congregate at Prickly Petey's quite frequently, I am told. What I haven't been able to ascertain is who hired the heathens. Someone paid a hefty sum of money to have you shot. Honestly, Harry, I am surprised whoever did pay these men has let them live this long, seeing as they let *you* live. You will probably want to talk to them soon, my heavy-hitting friend, as talking may be a skill these men cease to possess in the near future."

"Okay, thanks, Dudee, as always. We'll go track these shitbricks down and see what they can tell us, before someone put em outta our misery. In the meantime, maybe see if you can find anything about, like, chemicals, monsters, mutations, I dunno. The weirder the shit, the better, cause it seems like this case is goin further and further off the deep end."

"All right, Master Ypsilanti, safety and swiftness in your mission. I will relay anything I find to you immediately. It was lovely to meet you, young PI-in-training Lorene. I hope I will have the pleasure of your company again soon." Dudeford bows dramatically and reaches as if to kiss Lorene's hand. She pulls it back quickly, clearing her throat.

"Yep."

* * *

Neither Harry nor Lorene says anything for a long while inside the battered car, both lost in thought strands, working through everything that has happened to them over the last few days, thinking about what they might be wading into. Harry flips the radio on without looking at it, almost absentmindedly.

"—And so, as I said earlier, be alert when eating at the new 'fast food' restaurant, as the owners call it, and always bring an extra hunting knife, just in case. In other news, a house fire has claimed the life of a local woman today. Melinda Arnheim was asleep in her bed when a faulty television started the blaze, which quickly consumed the house. Ms. Arnheim was 88 years old. On a lighter note, town librarian Esther Wallace found a rare notebook belonging to —"

"Holy Jesus-jumpin-tha-bed! Granny Arnheim! Kid, it ain't no coincidence, her house burnin down like that!"

"Yeah, obviously, Harry. I'm sure whoever's behind this did it to cover up what happened to her. Maybe she was some kind of…test. See how it works, collect some data…then torch the place."

"Or maybe it was a trap to get us, kid. If someone's been keepin tabs on our progress with this case, day hadda know we'd be headin over ta Granny Arnheim's when we did. They knew it was our last lead. Either way, this shit-pool is about ta get a whole lot deeper. Listen, kid, if you wanna sit this one out, cool your heels at home, I get it. We'll probably be headed for a whole world a hurt, either them er us, ya hear me? Shit could go to a real dark place real quick. I picked up a few things bustin Nazi heads wit dem OSS boys, back in the war, and I ain't afraid to try an remember some of it, I need be. You'd be surprised just how many different pieces a tha human body got nerve endings capable of causin pain. I ain't exactly proud a it, kid, but if this show turns mean… I'm right there with it, grittin my fangs, laughin at tha blood and tha fields fulla body parts—laughin at death itself, right?! But *you* ain't gotta, kid. Not if you don't want to. I don't blame ya if ya don't."

Lorene looks solemnly at Harry. She is a bit shaken by his little speech; there is a crazed intensity in his eyes that tells her he isn't all talk and bluster, but something broken and pained in there as well. Tinge of pity for Harry, and for those saps that he was going to take that pain out on. As stupid as she feels thinking it, for the first time she feels sorry for Harry. "This is my fight too. I'm not just going to sit on the sidelines while you go face down danger! Besides, this job is finally getting exciting!"

"What, pullin cats outta trees and rectal tentacles don't rev yer engine? You kids nowadays, so hard ta please." Harry smiles at Lorene.

"C'mon, Harry. Let's go get our hands dirty."

10

LORENE DOESN'T LIKE the look of the town's miniature golf course as they pull up in front of it. Too colorful and bright. Too quiet. Too still. It feels like a bad old photo or tattered postcard.

"I don't like the look a this place, kid. Somethin feels funny," Harry says, echoing Lorene's inner monologue.

"Do you ever?"

"Heh, you got a point there, kid. Well, no sense in dawdlin."

***

"What exactly am I looking at here?" Lorene asks, more perplexed than disgusted at the carnage spread around the open area. Pieces where they shouldn't be. Bad imitations of what were once bodies. Solid shapes. The windmill turning slowly, sprayed and stuck with organic bits. Blood like dropped pain, like set dressing. Like too much salad dressing. Eyes seem as if they are still looking at the detectives, yet unfocused, like a painting that follows you from anywhere you gaze on it. Statue of Liberty waving her arm, sending slops of tendons and broken muscle and thickening blood.

"I...I honestly don't know, kid. I thought what I had in mind to do to em was bad. This...this is fucked right outta the park."

"Harry..."

"Uh-huh?"

"Can we get the fuck out of here?"

"Yeah, kid. I second that. We gotta go find that numbnuts Chief Dick-O. We might be into somethin over our heads here. Let's start back at Tom's, regroup, see if that chum bucket shows up again..."

II

"WELL, THAT'S...THAT'S a new ambiance, isn't it?" Harry says quietly. Lorene nods in agreement. The diner's windows seem to be fogged up or filmed over, the only thing visible inside a number of dark shapes moving about rapidly.

"I mean, it looks like they're just going about their business, maybe?" Lorene half asks, half states.

"Maybe. Guess there's only one way ta find out, huh?" Harry steps out of the car, pistol raised, and Lorene follows suit. A woman rounds the corner of the diner and Harry shrieks, leveling his weapon at her. Skin grey, twinkling with pustules and drool, thick slime. Hair pours from her scalp in clumps. Membranes wrinkling, splitting, gurgling as they collapse, like a Van Gogh made of cow cud and overripe strawberries. Truncated wrinkled lips cracking and flaking off, tongue a sock stuffed with rancid beans. Juiced organs leak between gaps in flesh. Pieces of animal cropping up dogsbody and crow. A smell like gasoline and poisoned wheat wafting off her.

"Wait, Harry, don't shoot!" Lorene barks. Harry glances at her but keeps his Colt trained on the woman, who has stopped a few feet away and is staring terrified at the pistol. "Annie?!" Lorene asks, stepping forward slowly.

"Lorene?! Hey, how are you doing? You out solving mysteries? So this must be your new boss, nice to meet you," Annie says, a small trail of slime leaking from her right eye and running down her cheek.

"Annie, are you...all right?"

"Oh yeah! Well, no... I mean, no, I don't think I am, actually. Kind of not all right at all, in fact..." Annie looks down at the pulpy, scaly puddles her hands have become.

"Well, uh..."

"Yeah. So, I'm sure you're super busy, not looking like a giant monster and all... Me, this is kind of—I'm kind of fixated on *this* right now. Just working through some things, finding some stuff out about myself. I was supposed to go on a date tonight, with Chet Chandling, but now... I don't know how I could pull it off looking like this. Plus, I just have this strange urge to pop someone's head off and suck the juices out like a big ol' crawdaddy!" Annie laughs at this, a sound that begins as hers but becomes a screaming chorus of broken voices, primordial agony, nature's fury. Lorene and Harry look around. Annie smiles at them. "Oh, don't worry, not you two. I was thinking I would go find that little Parrington kid, the one who always poops in my tomato garden. Maybe I'll see how easily *his* head comes off."

"Oh, yeah, Annie. That's… Yeah…"

"Well, it was, you know, good seeing you…if I could see… Just kind of sensing things with this, like, bat-radar thing. So that's an interesting twist on all this. You know, liven my day up a bit… But hey, we should get some coffee sometime, catch up."

"Oh yeah, Annie, definitely."

"Maybe we'll go get burgers and milkshakes; the whole vegetarian thing is out, on account of my new-found taste for human flesh, so…"

"Oh, good, I mean, uh, that's too bad about the diet part, but good about the lunch date. Just the girls…"

"Or girls and girl-monsters, if I'm stuck like this. I'm kinda becoming multi-sexed, I think. Definitely have a penis growing where a tail would be. That just started, so…"

"Oh, okay, yeah… Just, uh, the two of us. Well, Harry and I are looking into things so, you know, don't lose hope."

"Yeah… Yeah, hope kind of went out the window when these weird flappy tentacles shot out of my head. But if you two figure out a way to turn me back, don't you forget to let me know. I'll just be around here, probably collecting meat pieces to form into like a cocoon-type deal… You know, shed this skin and morph into an even more disgusting and mind-shreddingly monstrous butterfly… I might see if I can mobilize the cats of the neighborhood to get revenge on little Jimmy Parrington. That might be fun."

"Oh, we will. You'll be the first to hear if we find anything out. Take care with the whole—with, uh, everything. Maybe, uh, try not to dwell on it," Lorene stutters.

"Oh, yeah, already forgot about it. Like, *grr*, what hideous mutation, right?"

All three laugh, Lorene and Harry nervously. As Annie does, a boil erupts on her face, chowder in old rubbers, and a small tentacle wriggles out, shakes, sprouts a tiny face in the same manner Granny Arnheim's did, and begins laughing along with the group in tiny squeaks.

"Okay, see you later then," Lorene says, turning away quickly. With their backs to Annie, Harry gives Lorene a questioning look. Lorene shrugs.

"Onward and upward, Harry." She presses open the door and steps insides, pistol first.

* * *

There is no jukebox playing, no record skips, but the way the entire diner grows silent and turns toward Harry and Lorene in one swift motion, Lorene thinks she hears one in her head. An echoing moment before the silence, but maybe it was just her own heartbeat.

All the faces are looking up at them. All of them off, shifting as if in the shadow of a campfire or candle, yet the bright lights of Tom's are as painfully brilliant as ever. Lorene can't help a stifled half-gasp of terror.

Flailing tentacles like a mass of string or electrified worms. Hissing and the sound of wet scales slapping lino floors. Dishes knocked over. Some of the townspeople seem to be leaking green fluid in thick batter across tabletops, down their tattered pants and skirts, in streaks up the walls. Bubbles float and pop, sick and green, pale in the harsh light of the diner. Food dribbles and burps from their mouths. They stand, they creak, slick and dry-rotted at the same time.

A burst of energy, and all bodies are in motion, including Harry and Lorene's. Harry fires a couple quick shots into the nearest person, receiving a splash of incandescent green in response and little else. The creature continues toward him, and Harry raises the revolver into the air and brings it down on top of the creature's still vaguely human-looking head. It falls motionless to the ground in a heap, green goo splattering every direction. Lorene fires at one of the creatures as well, with similarly lackluster results. Harry and Lorene leap behind the counter, aiming at the approaching horde but not wasting ammo on firing.

"Any bright ideas, Harry?" Lorene asks.

"I don't think we brought the right firepower for this, kid. Maybe we sneak out the back and lock tha door behind us?"

"Okay. I'm completely on-board with that one. This place is a shitshow."

"Great. C'mon." Harry empties his weapon into the nearest creature, with Lorene following suit, staggering the mutated townspeople backward only briefly. Harry and Lorene duck into the kitchen and round a corner to find a tall older man holding a sawed-off shotgun. He fires, missing Harry and Lorene, hitting a bag of sweet potatoes behind them and sending chips of orange into the air. Harry slaps the weapon out of the man's hand.

"Goddamn it, Tom, you coulda hurt someone! Who the hell gave you a piece?"

"It was my granmama's, Harry, and I'm sorry, I thought you were one of them...things!"

"We ain't, but der right behind us, Tom! We gotta get the hell outta here, let's hit the back door and—"

"Can't hit the back door, Harry, it's sealed up."

"What da hell do ya mean, sealed up? What does that even mean?" A crash from behind them as the creatures begin pushing through the kitchen doors. Lorene fires at them and Harry dumps the empty shells from his revolver.

"C'mon, my office is secure, that's where we went when this all started."

The three race around a corner and in the direction of a closed door at the end of the short hall.

"Tom, it looks closed."

"Yeah, Harry. Okay, Edie, open it up! Code word: *Galoshes!*"

The door flies open, and a young woman stares out at them, terrified. The trio races inside, and the young woman slams the door shut behind them, tossing the lock to the sound of other bodies slamming into it. Hideous noises from just the other side. Breaking teeth and bursting udders. Sounds of sausage against salt licks. A groggy laugh from behind the thick metal door like gargling glass and spitting spoiled milk through the nose.

"Holy God," Harry huffs in between ragged breaths.

"Thanks," Lorene says to Tom. The tall man nods to her.

"Okay, Tom, now why the hell can't we get out tha back door? You said somethin about it bein sealed up? Tha fuck does that mean, pal?"

"Look, Harry, I dunno what to tell you. I tried em, neither of em would budge. Both of em were unlocked, made sure of it. My thinking is one of these things is blocking it or barricaded it up or something," Tom says wearily. He clutches the shotgun to his chest.

"Or the person who made these things. Why do I get the feeling we're being used in some kind of battle-readiness test, Harry?"

"Yeah, kid, I'm getting some serious flashbacks. This is smellin more an more like some evil Nazi-type shit the deeper we step in it."

"That means someone had to be here, with some kind of remote, to set it off, right when everything happened."

"You mean, a remote control?" Edie asks timidly. She is dressed in all black except a white blouse with thick grey stripes across it. She holds a notebook and seems remarkably calm for being so young. "Like the one my father has for his television?"

"Yes, exactly! Did you see someone with one?" Lorene asks excitedly. Outside the door, the noise of the crowd has died down.

"Yeah, I saw the guy who had it. Wrote a description of him down in my notebook, just before…everything." Edie picks up her notebook and flips a few pages in. "Tall man, large chest, wonder what his cock looks like under his tight pants—"

"C'mon now, is that really necessary?!" Tom interrupts, blushing a beet red.

Edie continues without acknowledging him. "Too nice clothes for this town, not from around here, too clean-cut. Tom hollers out another order, man picks his way toward bathroom, doesn't go in. Strange man, strange movements, too deliberate. I watch him as he pulls some kind of box from his jacket, looks like the remote control Bourgeois father has attached to TV. Alienated man comes home to wife and kids but says nothing. We watch from across the kitchen table, waiting for him to even acknowledge—"

"Hey, hey, c'mon now, focus. Any other details? Anything distinctive you noticed or wrote down, something to give us any kind of lead other than 'tall man, large chest, well dressed'?" Lorene asks.

"Um… Yeah, here. Doesn't return to table, as he turns to exit I see a scar running up his neck and to the edge of his beard. He presses a button on the box as he leaves. I reach for my coffee again— That's it. That's when everything started."

"Holy shit, Harry! I saw this guy! That day by the, um, movie theater, you know…that first day…" Lorene tries to give Harry a knowing look.

"Oh, you mean tha day we smoked grass, kid? Over by the movie theater?"

It's Lorene's turn to blush. Tom looks at her with disappointment but says nothing. Edie smirks.

"Yeah. I saw a man behind the movie theater that day that had a large scar like that, I saw it plain as day."

"What the hell were they doin behind the movie theater?"

"I don't know. Maybe we should start there, if we get out…"

"Not if, kid, when. The real question is… What's causin everyone else to mutate, but not the four of us?" Harry asks.

"That is strange. Harry and I found someone else, um, mutated… Melinda Arnheim… And so far we've been fine. So it's probably not airborne, or if it is, we must have an immunity or something. What do we all have in common that none of the others do?"

The group goes through so many factors, stuck in the cramped little office, beneath the naked bulb that brightened and turned a warmer shade of orangeish-yellow as if revving up, occasional sounds from outside reassuring them at least one of those things was still out there, waiting. Blood type. Age. Cigarette consumption. Weight and height. Drugs used. Drugs never used. When Harry starts to bring up sex, Tom and Lorene protest, while the young poet blushes and drops her eyes to the floor, a grin spreading her lips for just a moment. Illnesses…any recent? Ever had chicken pox? Measles? Scurvy?

"Food? Anything we all eat that would, you know, maybe give us some kind of immunity?" Lorene asks, hopeful. There aren't many other avenues to explore.

Not much in common. Coffee all around, but the same went for most of the creatures outside that door, back when they had been just normal paying customers. Harry, Tom, and Lorene all like pie. Edie does not. "Supplements? Vitamins? Anything?"

"What about things we don't eat? I can't stand Brussels sprouts, anybody else hate Brussels sprouts?" Harry asks. Edie raises her hand, not looking up from her notebook, scribbling frantically. "Okay, just one. What about beets? I can't stand beets either!" Edie raises her hand again. Tom and Lorene just look at Harry. "Well? What about you two, you two eat beets?"

"Not really, as far as I can say, I guess," Tom says.

"I don't think I've ever eaten a beet in my life Harry, but—"

"Ahah! Beets! That's it? None a us eats beets, none a us turns into a monster, I got it figured out!"

"Harry, I don't think half the people out there have eaten a beet in the last year or two, if ever, so it's not *that*," Lorene says, a little too harshly, and Harry looks hurt.

"Hell, I dunno. This is just a wild goose chase… Wait, goose!" Harry bellows.

Lorene narrows her eyes at Harry, then remembers the strange vats she saw being unloaded behind the movie theater that day; the van marked *Forest Rapids Meat Packing Plant*. "Harry, you might be onto something. What about meat! I told you about those men I saw at the theater. Well, the van they were unloading from was marked *Forest Rapids Meat Packing Plant*. So…red meat, maybe?"

"I only eat toast and coffee. That's it," Edie says, matter-of-factly.

"Even at home?"

"At home I eat the occasional piece of fish, but it's mostly just the same. I am a tool for art."

"Uh, great. Tom?"

"My doctor made me stop eating red meat, for my heart. And I haven't broken my word to him yet. The word between a man and his doctor is a sacred bond," Tom says.

"Well, I haven't eaten red meat in months, I've been trying to help my friend Annie out with her vegetarian diet," Lorene says, looking as if she is sharing some shameful secret though she doesn't know why.

"Wait, you mean *Annie*, the friend we saw out there with all the pus and slime and RAARRRRGH! Screaming tentacles and such? I guess we can rule out this theory too," Harry says.

"Not necessarily. Annie wasn't always the best with self-control. Like I said, I was trying to help her, by giving her a strong example. But I think she broke her diet on more than a few occasions."

"Little Annie McFreeson, Chucky and Darla's girl? She would sneak in here early on Sunday mornings while everyone was still in church, and she'd have me cook her up a big plate a bacon. She looked like a right wild animal," Tom says, chuckling to himself.

"Okay. So, Harry, what about you?"

"Well, I mostly just eat MRES at home. Happened to, uh, *procure* a full truck load of em, so, you know, ain't gotta go grocery shoppin much anymore. If I'm out I'm eatin here, and lately I been gettin Tom's fox burger… Is fox red meat? I think it is," Harry asks. Tom and Lorene look at each other in confusion.

"Harry, I don't have a *fox* burger," Tom says.

"Yeah, it's the one I get every time I come in here, the one you said was healthier and leaner. You told me it was the one you always eat now. Man, slap some extra pickles and hot sauce on dat puppy…best damn burger I ever had in my life. Hands down."

"The *faux-burger*, Harry? The beans and grains one Tom makes?" Lorene asks.

"Yeah, *fox*, like that fancy French way a writin it, you know," Harry says. Edie looks up from her notebook, her pen stopped mid-word, and stares at Harry for a moment before bursting into laughter.

"Holy shit, Harry," Lorene says.

"Boy, you are some kinda dense, aren't you? The faux burger isn't meat—especially not fox! You been eatin beans and grains for over a year and a half now, just like me!" Tom laughs and slaps Harry on the back. Harry looks upset for a moment, and then a smile draws across his unshaven face.

"Huh. I'll be damned. Still da best goddamn burger I ever ate. Huh…ya learn somethin new every day…"

"Don't you see, Harry? What if the meat's the key? Annie was still in partial control of herself because she was only eating it when she cheated, so she must have gotten much less of whatever it is they're putting in it."

"Tom, where do you get your meat?" Harry asks.

"Well, uh, my burger and pork I've been getting from that Forest Rapids Meat Market over there on Oak. They're just such a better price than anywhere else."

"Kid, what say we get outta here, and we put your theory to the test, go see if we can't take a tour a that meat packin plant over there?"

"That sounds good, Harry. I assume that means you have a plan for getting us out of here?"

"Uh, kinda, kid. Hope I do. Tom, which wall is the outside one?"

"This one. Why, Harry? What are you fixing to do?"

"These walls is that drywall gypsum stuff, right? I'm fixin, Tom, to make us a door right on out to the parking lot. Unless you got a better idea?"

"No, no, I don't. Just, you know, try not to do any more damage than you gotta. I don't think my insurance covers alien invasion, or whatever y'all say this is."

"Don't worry, Tom, just a little hole, and we should be waltzin on outta here."

* * *

Harry fires the shotgun into the wall, smoke from the weapon mingling with white powder misting into the air. Two large fist-sized holes and daylight rains in. Lorene smells gunpowder singing on the air. Burnt rock and paper. Tom's bad cologne. And something else.

Edie and Tom plug their ears as Harry raises the shotgun again, and Lorene follows suit. Two more explosions muffled through Lorene's sweaty fingers. The crashing against the door increases; Lorene thinks she sees the hinges shudder violently with each blow.

"Harry, we gotta speed this up, I don't think that door is going to hold much longer," Lorene says, trying to keep the panic from creeping into her voice.

"I'm trying the best I can, kid. We only got one big gun, our little popguns ain't gonna even hardly do nothin to it. Fire in the hole!"

Harry pulls both triggers again and rips another jagged chunk from the wall, now with a large wound across its center. Warm air from outside pours in. Another rush of scent, Lorene looks around, suddenly realizes what she's smelling.

"I smell gas! Does anyone else smell gas?!"

Tom and Edie begin sniffing the air as Harry reloads the shotgun.

"Last bullets. Almost there…"

"Harry, I don't know if that's such a good idea…"

"I smell it too!" Edie chimes in.

"Okay, everyone, get against this far wall. We ain't got much choice, I'm gonna try an ram it first, but if that don't work, I gotta put these last slugs through it. Two more holes might just be enough."

Harry takes a few steps backward across the room and readies himself. He takes off at a surprising speed, and lowers his shoulder as he throws his entire weight into the battered wall. It shakes, Harry grunts in pain and bounces off, but the wall holds true.

"Goddamnit. Okay, everyone, hold onto somethin!" Harry bellows, raising the shotgun and pulling the first trigger, cutting one side of the wall away. He lines up the next one and fires, blowing away the final chunk holding a large section of the wall on. A thunderous sucking sound erupts, and Harry turns to see a flame hovering in the air around the door behind him. Before even turning around, before even processing what he is saying, he shouts, "Run!" and turns to see the group already pushing their way through the jagged gap outside. His legs have already begun moving and his body diving for the opening when a force from behind him lifts him into the air and forward. Heat and tingling; as he is tossed through the broken drywall, everything goes black.

12

"HARRY! HARRY, WAKE up! Harry, c'mon, big guy… That's it…"

Harry stirs, and sits upright in a bolt of quivering meat. He looks himself over, then back at the ruined wall of the diner he'd been flung through.

"You okay?" Lorene asks, looking back over Harry's flight path. A few patches of his jacket are blackened, he has a spot of road-rash scraping up his right arm and under the coat, but it doesn't look too bad. Harry moves his limbs and other pieces, feeling across himself for damage.

"Yeah, kid, I think so. Prolly a few bruises, a few cuts…prolly gonna need a new jacket, but… Yeah, I think so. Any of those things make it out?"

"Not as far as we can tell, we've been keeping a pretty close eye on the front door. Sirens are getting close, so the cops'll be here soon, whether that's good or bad," Lorene says flatly, and gives a half-smile.

"Hey, kid, don't worry, I'm fine. Don't go startin to get all soft on me now."

"Actually, Harry, I'm still trying to process what the fuck just happened in there…to *me*. I'm glad you're okay, but *I* almost bit it back there too. I don't think I've ever had quite that kind of experience," Lorene says, looking back at the diner with a mix of revulsion and intense curiosity.

"Fair enough, kid. This is goin pretty far beyond my on-the-job experiences for me, too. Offer's on the table still… I can leave you here with Tom and the beatnik and you can fill the coppers in on the monster movie we just saw goin on in there. I wouldn't hold it against ya. You already helped out more'n you needed to…ain't no reason both of us gotta face these nightmares."

"I already told you, Harry, I don't have anything better to do. Besides, someone has to look after you when you do something stupid like blow up the room you're standing in."

"Okay, gotta make a stop first, at my place," Harry says, smiling a little at Lorene.

"You mean I'll get to see the place the legendary Harry Ypsilanti calls home? And to what do I owe this great honor?"

"Uh, yeah, you might not be seein it just yet, kid, place is a mess and…if you don't mind, I'll just run in by myself. We're stoppin there just ta get some some extra firepower. We're gonna need more'n just these little popguns if we gonna go all Davy Crockett on these creeps."

"Sure, Harry. Don't want me to see your dirty undies?"

"Yeah, somethin like that."

* * *

Lorene begins to grow impatient sitting in the car outside Harry's small ranch-style home. Even with all the windows rolled down, sweat rivets and gallops down Lorene's body. She shakes her head and curses Harry under her breath.

The heavy thump of the bag Harry drops in the car's backseat scares her for a moment. Gunmetal and bullet boxes peek out. Harry asks her if she's ever shot anything besides a pistol, and she tells him she shot her father's rifle a few times.

"Good," he says, and he pulls an M-1 from the satchel and hands it to her.

"Doesn't the army need this?"

"Nah, they making new guns nowadays…machine guns, fire ten times as fast as this old relic," Harry replies. "But they all plastic bullshit, fall apart first guy's head you knock with em." He pulls a .30-06 rifle and a sawed-off shotgun from the bag. "I think these two're mine. Let's go find out just who's fuckin with our town."

* * *

Headlights across bodies in the darkness. Shapes flittering in all directions like shadows fleeing a light just flicked-on. Lorene can't make out any faces as the group scatters, just the promise of bodies and swift departure. Cockroaches scurrying under kitchen appliances and bathroom sinks.

"The hell is goin on here?" Harry asks. He quickly rolls his window down and yells, "Hey, where's everybody goin, we brought party favors!"

Three men are left in the brightness of the car's lights as Harry turns off the engine and opens his door.

"Good evening," one of the men, dressed in coveralls stained with red and brown streaks, says. Lorene steps out of the car too, slowly, hand on the weapon tucked under her jacket.

"How's it goin, pal? Me and my friend here just saw the gatherin, looked like you kids was havin tons o fun over here, thought we might come on over and join ya… If it isn't too forward, ya know."

"I'm afraid this is a private event, in fact, so if you don't mind—"

"Kinda do mind, friend-o. Kinda do. It's just, I never got me no parties when I was a kid, my parents always seemed to forget about my birthday, and—" Harry begins.

"Drop the fucking shtick, PI. We know who you are."

"Oh, good, cause I wasn't really sure where I was goin wit dat one. So, you know who I am, maybe we start, you tell us who you are. Maybe why the fuck you're turnin people round my city inta crazy monsters?"

"Over catastrophe shudder the victors of time."

"The fuck does that even mean? You get what the fuck dat means, kid?"

"No, Harry, I have no idea…but I'm guessing it's not good."

"No, prolly not, kid. Okay, look, I might get what yer steppin in, but my partner here, she's a little new to the whole detectin game. Maybe help her out, give it to us in real people talk, you know, sensicle stuff, not…uh, well, cult-crazy gibberish."

The man begins laughing slowly, eerily. Lorene doesn't want to take her eyes from him, but notices one of the other men is gone. She peers behind herself briefly, seeing the man approach the gate they had driven through and throwing a lock.

"Uhh, Harry, I think we're locked in."

"I saw that, kid. So, mister bigshot, let's speed this up. What's the point of all this? World domination? Revenge fer bein picked on as a kid? I get that, I was bullied in fourth grade, before I grew inta myself, they used ta call me Hopeless Harry. Did ya mommy not breastfeed you enough? Did she breastfeed you too much?"

"Maybe he's being paid to test some new military technology…or maybe it's a super-virus that's gotten out of control!"

"Oh, no, I know, maybe it's—"

"Shut the fuck up, you moronic fucking gumshoes! Just shut the fuck up! Especially you, Yapsongdoodie, er, Yacka, uh—"

"Yp-si-lan-ti. *Yip-see-lan-tea.* That's it."

"Whatever! There is no point to this, no point to any of this! You don't need to figure it out, you'll be fucking dead soon enough! You think you—"

Before the man can finish his sentence, Lorene pivots, pulling the revolver from beneath her coat and firing at the man who had locked the gate and was still lingering behind them. She hits him and he calls out for a brief moment, a quiet thud as he goes silent.

"What was that bout us bein dead soon?" Harry quips. Lorene fires a few more times, hitting both of the other henchman. Harry is delighted.

"Anyway, continue your story, sorry to interrupt."

"Kid, that was a good one! Yer gettin tha hang a this thing!"

The man laughs again, a sound of broken pipes gurgling and sputtering, a sound of bricks pinging dully off each other. Harry sighs heavily and fires at the man, hitting him in his left knee and dropping him instantly. The man screams an incomprehensible mix of tongues and curses.

"Okay, pal, how about we try this again. Hi, my name's Harry Ypsilanti. PI. Yep, it's a weird one, don't sweat it if you don't get it right the first time, most people don't. But by the time I'm through with ya, you'll remember it, that's for sure. This is my partner, Lorene. We got some questions for ya, maybe ya got tha time ta answer them?"

"That was the last big mistake you'll make, gumshoe. You shoulda shot me in the head instead of yapping your fat mouth." The wounded man pulls one of the radio transmitter devices from his coat.

"Hah, we already figured out yer scheme, dipshit, and neither of us eats red meat. Sorry, you ain't got no one ta turn inta mutants, unless maybe ya wanna mutate yerself," Harry bellows at the man triumphantly.

"Ha… HAHAHAHAHA!!! Great job, PI, you sure got it all figured out…except, of course, that the pathogen doesn't just work on living flesh. Any exposed flesh will do. But how would you figure that out, right?" He presses the button, and a small red light illuminates on the box in his hand.

All around them a rumbling. Wet and bassy. Chicken pieces slapping around the inside of rainsticks. Crates shake. Terrifying moaning from another room. Clanking like footsteps but more like dropping air-sick bags off awnings.

"Harry…"

"Yeah, kid?"

"I think we fucked up again."

"Yeah, this might be bad, kid."

"Might be? It certainly fucking is, PI! This will be your—" The man is cut off as his head explodes upward, spraying the railing behind him and raining down onto the catwalk below. Harry lowers the rifle.

"Harry, he might be the only person who can stop this! Why the hell did you shoot him?!"

"That fuckin whack-job weren't gonna tell us nothin. Might as well take him off our worry list first thing, that's what I say. That's what I said in the war too, but nobody listened to me."

"Great thinking, Harry," Lorene spits sarcastically. "What about the rest of the pack?" She points at the figures moving swiftly toward them out of the darkness. Footsteps like zombie movies, but wetter. As they reach the light, Lorene sees they are clearly chunks of meat, mutated, moving swiftly. Some are full slices of animals, halves of cows with tentacles and spider legs and gnashing mouths. Whole plucked chickens bouncing wetly, oozing and shrieking, waving pincers, eyeballs where there shouldn't be. There are things that look like they have already been decomposing before mutating, collections of scraps and garbage, spoiled meat breathing as if it has lungs, hissing hoarsely, something like a tongue darts out, licks what Lorene sees as lips and wishes she hadn't. Other clumps of things Lorene's brain can't unpack, slime and hair and gristle, screaming, wavering like Jell-O under skin that might just be crust. Lorene can't help herself as she screams along.

"Let's fall back to that little office right when we came in. Move!" Harry and Lorene run full-bore back the way they had entered the plant, twisting around a number of crates, machines, metal gates, and fences, the sound of the flesh that chases them growing louder as it increases speed, closing the gap. *We're not gonna make it...* Lorene's brain flashes briefly.

"Harry, I'm gonna turn around and lay down some cover fire, you do the same with the shotgun! We gotta slow em down!" Lorene yells up at him, tactical advice from somewhere deep inside she can't place. She whirls around and drops to her knee, raising the rifle and firing in a series of motions far smoother than she would have believed she was capable of in that moment. She fires, aims, fires again, repeating until the jarring sound of empty metal slapping metal and no report of car collision from the barrel. She jumps up and begins running as fast as she can push her legs. "Harry, now!"

Harry spins and unloads both barrels of the shotgun into the approaching horde, exploding one slab of something about the size of a small child, sending gore spraying across the remaining group. Lorene slaps a new clip into the rifle just like Harry showed her and drops back to her knee. She fires five shots in quick succession, unsure how many things she hits but seeing sprays of gore as positive affirmation. The horde falls back as Harry and Lorene take off running again.

"Almost there, kid, you get inside, I'll give em one more taste—"

Lorene leaps through the door and Harry fires one barrel, then the second, tossing a pair of flapping Cornish hens flying back into the looming wall of meat and quivering fangs and shrieking. Harry dives backward, and Lorene slams the door, which falls forward and into the hallway they just entered from.

"Shit!"

"Harry, the bathroom!" Lorene shouts, and the two dive inside as the horde breaches the small office and begins flooding in. Lorene throws the small lock and steps back from the door, rifle half-raised. Harry squats next to her, quickly reloading the shotgun and then raising it at the ready, tensely watching the door as well. Thumps and crashes. Screams from the other side. The door shakes; the wall around it seems to shimmer and sway with every blow from outside. Howling and splashing slaps. The noises continue for uncounted moments, tense breaths and sweating palms on gunmetal and wood. Fingers hover over triggers. Finally the sounds subside. Silence from the other side of the door.

"Well, this feels familiar."

"They ain't gone, that's sure as shit."

"No, they're definitely up to something, aren't they?"

"You're the smart one. Any brilliant ideas on how we get outta here?"

"I have no idea. You got anything?"

"Not really, kid. I ain't even got any semi-witty one-liners. Maybe I can rush out there, distract enough of dem things so you can escape, maybe…"

"That's not much of a plan."

"You come up with a better one, I'm all ears, kid. Please, come up with a better one. I dare ya."

"You don't happen to have anything explosive on you, do you?"

"No."

"Wait, Harry, I might have an idea…and this one might actually work without one of us sacrificing ourselves for the other. You remember when they made a big deal last year about installing that brand new cooling system, they called it 'liquid nitrogen cooling,' brought in a big tank to keep it in, had all these safety trainings and press conferences and demonstrations and everything? It can freeze a full chicken in a few seconds, they said…turn it as brittle as a snow cone. If we can get em close enough to that tank, it's goodbye Monday Mystery Meat…"

"Okay, how the fuck do we do that?"

"That old Harry Ypsilanti magnetism you keep talking about, of course."

"Oh, Jesus. We're gonna die, ain't we?"

* * *

It doesn't take Harry long to find the large, gleaming tank. Looming up above the other more battered and worn-out fixtures of the plant, Harry sees it at the back of the building, past the piles of meat and flayed bodies that are still bobbing and loitering around the entrance to the office Lorene and Harry are holed-up in.

"You ready, kid?" Harry asks, tossing the cigarette he'd just lit onto the concrete.

"I don't think so, but does it matter?"

"Nah, not really."

"Okay, so… You run out screaming like a maniac, run them over past it, when I hear the signal I shoot at the tank and shut the door. That's it."

"Kinda seems like a half-plan, don't it?"

"Well, it's this or try to blow another hole in the wall, and this building is a little more solid than Tom's. So, y'know…hang onto something."

Harry raises the shotgun and turns toward the door, taking a long breath before reaching for the cold metal handle.

"Harry…"

Harry turns back to Lorene. "Huh?"

"Try not to die out there. I really don't want to have to find another job." Lorene forces a terse smile.

"Sure thing, kid. And if I don't make it…"

"Yeah?"

"Torch my place for me, will ya? I don't want my family goin through it after I'm gone."

"Sure, Harry."

"I mean it. You're the only one I can trust with that."

"Be careful."

* * *

The next few moments are a strange stuttering of blurry speed and draining slow-motion. Harry kicks the door open with as much noise as he can muster, leather sole on metal echoing around the concrete building. The hissing and screeching starts. Lorene loses Harry in a blur of movement, flare of shotgun blasts, blood and fluids spraying like wake as he skates toward the tank. Screaming—some from Harry, some from inhuman lips or mockeries of them. Harry taunting the things surrounding him, beckoning them behind a large stack of crates, out of Lorene's line of sight. Hours might have hummed by, or only a few nanoseconds between heartbeats. Lorene feels panic rise up as the noise of Harry and his ruckus cease, ragged breath shaking the rifle pressed to her shoulder. She stares over the wooden length, metal sight drawn dead set on the tank, ears playing tricks as she searches for anything to grasp.

A bellow rises out of the silence, the battering of gunshots, and Lorene pulls the trigger. Once, twice, three times, squeezing gently, gaining a feel for the kick of the rifle against her shoulder, one hole opening in the silver metal, then two, clear liquid rolling out of the wounds with plumes of steam, a third, and Lorene feels the rush of explosive force and the heat before she hears the explosion and realizes she is being thrown across the little office, sees the flash of light just before losing consciousness.

She feels lightness. She feels lifting. Worlds rage in and out of view. Lights as faces, as the flash of people. Heat across her arm, wavering moment of lucidity as she floats past burning crates, past the orange and sun-colored lick of flames, floating, eyes heavy as she slips back across streams of time and geography, sees her parents on Christmas morning, smiling and sipping the aromatic coffee they only brewed on special occasions. Sees her brother opening a toy horse wrapped in shiny red paper, the way his eyes light up as he begins to tear at the slick paper—

—Lorene's first kiss, the boy who'd taken her to prom, fumbling and awkward, but she still feels her heart race like she had just run into adulthood, chased an older version of herself down, merging her child-body with the elder one, taking over—

—and then she just sees night sky; not like here in the city, but the night sky of summers up north with her family, lying on the soft grass, feeling the heat still streaming from the earth into the cool dark air, washes of stars like paint pricks lit by the cool blue-white lamp of the moon. Millions of them, pixie swarms of them. Lorene tries to unfocus her eyes to see as many as she can at once, and at some point she slips quietly into the darkness around her.

* * *

"C'mon, aw Jesus, I see ya breathin still, c'mon, kid, you can't…you can't fuckin die on me, okay? Not here, not now! C'mon!" Harry's voice grows frantic. Lorene begins to wake, eyes still pressed closed, shadows surrounding her. Harry's hands shake her softly, and Lorene opens one eye, the other seeming like it's stuck shut.

"Kid, good, aw, you're alive! Here, here, don't move too much, give it a second, see if ya got anything broken or whatnot first… That cut above yer eye don't look too bad, might not be able to open it fer a day or two, but could be worse."

Harry raises his left hand, which is wrapped in a torn piece of fabric, stained with blood. Beneath, Lorene sees the shortened nubs of what were Harry's pinkie and ring fingers.

"Harry!"

"Yeah, this one's real dis time. Actually didn't really hurt much, but fuck-howdy I wasn't expectin that tank ta just go up like that. That's the second building we blown up in two days. Before I met you, I never blowed buildings up…so, uh, thanks, kid. Fer everything. I don't know if I would'a made it if you hadn'ta been here…"

"Thanks, Harry, for taking a chance on me."

"Chance, are you kidding me? Kid, you scored highest on that entrance exam to be a copper that anyone ever has. I wasn't kiddin when I said you was worth ten of Dickie Boy's dingleberries. You wanna smoke some grass, kid? I think I need me a toke or three…"

"Sure, Harry. I think I might just do that. I heard my boss might be giving me some vacation time here coming up, so I can do whatever I feel like…"

"Heh-heh, yeah. Yeah, I mean—not too much time, right? Cause this ain't over, you know, not by a long shot. You saw all them people meetin with that meat plant manager. Even if more'n half of em were bodyguards and henchmen, that's still a lotta other interests in whatever the fuck it is we just stumbled on. But for now, you earned your first RnR, kid. Earned it well." Harry lights the joint and takes a long, slow draw.

"Thanks, Harry. Give me a week, let me rest up, maybe write up a last will and testament, just in case… And when I come back, we blow this thing wide open. Can you survive a week without me?" Lorene takes the joint from Harry.

"Honestly, kid, right now, in this moment, I dunno if I can answer that question. But that's good, a week, we both need to cool our heels, lick our wounds, finish tha watercolor we been workin on fer tha last couple a months, then back to ass kickin…"

"Harry Ypsilanti, did you just admit to having a hobby?"

"Nah, kid, purely hypothetical…you know, metaphorical and what not…" Harry passes Lorene the joint.

"I wouldn't have taken you for the artist type. You're a man of many secrets, aren't you?"

"Yeah, kid, all of em ain't as endearin as paintin pretty flowers and landscapes, though. But hell, we all got secrets, don't we? I bet you got a few, locked away in the ol closet somewhere."

Lorene just smiles and nods, feeling the effect of the drug mingle with the concrete malt of fatigue sloshing through her system as she hits the joint again. She hands it back to Harry.

"I'll see you in a week?" she says, somewhere between a question and a statement.

"One week. Be careful out there, watch your back. And rest up, kid, you earned it. Goddamn did you earn it."

Lorene leaves Harry puffing away in the Piggly Wiggly parking lot, watching her walk in a shuffling daze toward her apartment building just up the road. She hears Harry's choking cough behind her, and the distinct sound of his laughter. Lorene can't help the smile that pulls itself across her face. *Not bad for the first week on the job*, she thinks. *Not bad at all.*

About the Author

Kyle Wright is the author of *In Control* (2021, Bizarro Pulp Press), *Videodrome*, and *mindfuck* (2018 and 2019, Really Serious Literature). His writing explores various genres and the flimsy boundaries between them. He currently lives in Chicago with his partner and their elderly cat. You can find him on Twitter, Instagram, and TikTok @montageculture.

www.ingramcontent.com/pod-product-compliance
Lightning Source LLC
Chambersburg PA
CBHW030356180626
46812CB00007B/2905